At last the bell went. Everyone who wanted was given a chance to try out for the course, so the football field was packed with children kicking balls around.

Finally, Mr Jay blew the whistle and everyone gathered round, panting and breathless.

'Well, kids!' he said, smiling. 'We've got a lot of young stars in this school. You've all worked hard and I'm really proud of you. But I'm afraid there's only one place on the Football Magic course, so those of you who aren't picked mustn't feel you've failed.'

I wish he'd just get on with it! thought Karen, impatiently. All she wanted was to know, one way or the other. Well, there was one other thing she wanted, of course!

'And so, the lucky person is . . . Karen,' said Mr Jay.

Karen stood there, her mouth open. She couldn't believe it. He'd picked her!

FOOTBALL MAGIC

E. DALE

CORGI YEARLING BOOKS

FOOTBALL MAGIC
A CORGI YEARLING BOOK : 0 440 863589

First publication in Great Britain

PRINTING HISTORY
Corgi Yearling edition published 1998

Copyright © 1998 by Elizabeth Dale
Chapter head artwork by Slatter-Anderson

Cover photo supplied by Coerver Coaching

Typeset in 13/15pt Century Schoolbook by
Phoenix Typesetting, Ilkley, West Yorkshire.

Corgi Yearling Books are published by
Transworld Publishers Ltd,
61-63 Uxbridge Road, Ealing, London W5 5SA,
in Australia by Transworld Publishers
(Australia) Pty. Ltd,
15-25 Helles Avenue, Moorebank, NSW 2170,
and in New Zealand by Transworld Publishers (NZ) Ltd,
3 William Pickering Drive, Albany, Auckland.

Made and printed in Great Britain by
Cox & Wyman Ltd, Reading, Berks.

For Katie, with love

CHAPTER 1

'Quick, Kaz, pass! To me!' screamed
Gary. 'Now!'

Karen paused in mid-run. Gary was
being marked by someone twice his size,
whereas she had a clear run to the goal.
She had to go for it. She chipped the ball
ahead, kept on running, drew back her
right foot and *wham*! As the ball went
sailing high into the back of the net,
Karen felt as though she could have
floated in after it. A goal! She'd scored a
goal! Everyone came and patted her on
the back; it was the most brilliant
moment of her life.

'Fantastic!' cried Dave.

'Nice one, Kazza!' said Spike, ruffling

her shoulder-length black hair.

Karen smiled at her mum and Suzie, who were madly jumping up and down on the touch-line. It was the most magical moment. To score a goal for her school team was one thing, but to score a goal in the final of the Inter-Schools Challenge Cup was something else!

As she ran back to the centre spot, Gary came running up to her. She grinned at him.

'Why didn't you pass it to me?' he snarled. 'I can't stand stuck-up girls who hog the ball in the hope that one day they might get round to scoring!'

She stared at him. 'I couldn't . . .' she began. 'I didn't . . .'

'Push off, Gary!' said Dave, who'd heard him. 'You're only jealous because she's better than you.'

'Girls shouldn't be allowed in the team,' said Gary. 'Everyone knows they only ever get the ball because some boys let them.'

The whistle blew and Karen was soon immersed in the game, all thoughts of Gary gone. There were only twenty minutes left; they were only one goal ahead – they mustn't let their guard slip. It was a hard match, and everyone was tired. Probably most tired of all was Karen's mum, she hadn't stopped yelling since the game started!

'Come on Garrett Street Middle School!' she called, as they went on one final attack. Spike passed the ball to Dave out on the wing; he ran, side-stepped the opposition, pushed it across to Karen – there was just the goalie between her and the open goal.

'Kazza!' cried Gary to her right. This time he was unmarked. She kicked it to him, he turned, aimed the ball at the net, and missed. Everyone groaned.

'Why didn't you shoot?' Spike yelled at her. 'Dave laid it on perfectly for you, you were in front of the goal, you had a brilliant chance and you passed it back out again to Gary. Are you chicken, or something?!'

'No!' said Karen, indignantly. How could she explain that she'd had her moment of glory, she'd wanted to let someone else have a triumph, too? Above all else, she wanted to be accepted as a proper part of the team. But the Forest goalkeeper had already kicked the ball up to the other end of the field, there was no time to argue.

There were another ten hectic, nail-biting minutes, in which it seemed absolutely certain that Forest School would score at least five goals, but somehow they kept missing. And then, at last, the final whistle blew. They'd won the Cup, and all thanks to Karen's goal!

Everyone hugged each other in glee. They were all talking at once, comparing experiences and congratulating each other, including the other team. For Karen, to be part of the team, to win, it was like Christmas and all her birthdays rolled into one. And then, as they all walked up to the table at the end of the pitch to collect the Cup, the most terrible thing happened. Karen could feel tears welling up in her eyes. She mustn't cry, she mustn't! Everyone would think she was a real drip! Quickly she wiped her sleeve across her eyes, and stood in line with the others as Spike, their captain, collected the Cup. Everyone cheered. Everyone, that is, except Karen's mum, whose voice had finally packed up. She was wiping her eyes, as though . . . no! She mustn't! Karen glared at her.

The Cup was passed round everyone, someone produced a camera, a reporter from the local paper wanted to know what Karen's name was, and then they all went in to get changed.

'I'm sorry I fluffed that chance you gave me to score again,' Karen said to Dave as they walked off the pitch.

'Oh that doesn't matter!' he said. 'You scored the first time, and we won, didn't we? That's all that counts!'

'Yes,' said Karen. 'It was a brilliant game!'

'Do you know,' said Suzie, 'when they handed Spike the Cup, I was so proud, I felt like bursting into tears, and I wasn't even in the team!'

Karen smiled at her, gratefully. She couldn't have admitted such a thing to anyone. 'How about coming round to my house afterwards?' she suggested, as Dave joined them. 'My mum's made a special celebration cake – and I could do with some help eating it.'

'How did she know we were going to win?' asked Dave.

'She didn't. If we lost she was going to give me a big piece to take with my lunch every day to make me feel better.'

'She's all right, your mum!' said Dave. 'I'm really glad we won.'

'So am I,' said Karen, pulling a face. 'You haven't tasted her cake, yet!'

The cake was actually one of Karen's mum's better efforts, which was a real shame, because Karen had invited the whole team round, as well as Suzie, to help her eat it up. Everyone came, except Gary.

'Don't worry about him,' said Steve. 'He's just sulking because he was only first reserve.'

'Yeah!' said Spike. 'He was really annoyed when you were picked to be in the team instead of him, Kaz. Do you know, he was even thinking of appealing against the result on the grounds that we had a girl in our team!'

'But you won!' exclaimed Suzie.

'I know,' said Spike. 'Just think what a fuss he'd have created if we'd lost!'

'Hey, have you heard about Football Magic?' asked Steve.

'Yeah, it's what we were today,' said Spike. 'Absolute magic!'

Everyone laughed.

'I know,' said Steve, 'but it's als

the name of a football training course they're running in the Easter holidays.'

'Really?' gasped Dave.

'Where?' demanded Spike.

'In Manchester. And someone from our school is going to get a place. There'll be special coaching and matches and expert training sessions. There's a notice on the board. There are going to be trials for it at school next week.'

'Wow!' exclaimed Karen. 'What I wouldn't give to go on that! How long does it last?'

'A week. But it costs eighty pounds.'

'Is that all?' said Karen. 'That's no problem, is it Mum?'

Karen's mum opened her mouth to argue, but only a croak came out.

'I wonder who'll be picked to go. Who wants another piece of cake?' asked Karen, happily.

CHAPTER 2

All anyone could talk about the next week was Football Magic and the forth-coming trials.

'Of course, Spike will win the place,' said Karen, as she and Dave walked to school. 'He's brilliant.'

'Well,' said Dave, 'he might not. After all, who would have given us a chance of winning the Cup at the beginning of this term? And we did. Maybe he'll have an off day when we have the trials?'

'Spike?!' exclaimed Karen. 'An off day?! Pigs might turn purple and fly up to the moon!'

But Spike looked as though he was having an off day when they saw him i the playground. He was on his own, kicking a stone around, and looking as though he wished it was his deadliest enemy.

'All right, Spike?' said Dave. 'Practising for the trials?'

'I'm not entering,' muttered Spike.

'What?!' gasped Karen. 'I think you have to enter, you know. They're not just going to give you a place because Mr Jay says you're totally brilliant!'

'I'm not going on the course,' said Spike. 'Would you believe that my parents had already booked for us to go skiing in Austria this Easter.'

'Wow!' said Karen. 'You lucky thing!'

'Hardly!' said Spike. 'I can't speak a word of German and I'm useless at skiing. I'm more likely to fall down the mountain on my first day, break my leg and both arms and be off football for the next six months! I'd much rather go to Football Magic.'

'What a shame,' said Dave, trying not to smile. 'Still it does give everyone else a chance at the trials, doesn't it? Come on, Kaz, let's get a ball and practise.'

All Karen seemed to do for the next few days was eat, sleep and play football.

'But, then,' said her mum, as she called her in to bed for the third time, 'what else did you ever do? You still haven't tidied your room this week and I asked you on Monday!'

'I haven't had time,' said Karen. 'But I promise you, Mum, if I get to go on this course, I'll tidy my room every day for a week!'

'It only needs tidying once!' called her mum after her as she went up to have a bath. 'Once it's tidy, it's tidy!'

'I always thought that if I had a little girl, she'd be playing with dolls and helping me to make cakes,' said her mum, as she helped to dry Karen's hair that night.

'But my cooking's just like yours!' said Karen. 'If I made cakes, too, we'd have twice as many that we'd have to eat up.'

'That's true!' said her mum.

'Anyway, football's such fun, Mum!' said Karen. 'Didn't you like it when you were a little girl?'

'I didn't get a chance to play it,' said her mum.

Karen stared at her. 'You never played

football!' she exclaimed, her eyes big and round.

'Oh, I kicked a ball around with my brother,' said her mum. 'But I never went out on a football pitch and played a real game. Girls didn't in my day.'

'I can't believe it!' said Karen. 'I mean, not having videos and computers and *Neighbours* when you were little, that's bad enough. But to have to do without football! You must have been really deprived!'

Her mum laughed. 'You'd better not let Gran hear you say that,' she said. 'Come on, let's get you to bed, you've got your trial tomorrow.'

Karen sighed. 'I wish I could have practised more. Some of the boys at school are so much bigger than me, they can head balls I can't even reach, and they can shoot harder.'

'Yes, but you can run faster than the lot of them!' said her mum. 'And you've got more determination than the rest of them put together. When you're standing in front of a goal with the ball between your feet, I'd rather die than be the goalkeeper.'

'I think I'll die if I don't get on the course,' said Karen.

'I'll make you a nice cake for you to eat in case you don't,' said her mum.

'Well, that settles it!' said Karen. 'I'm absolutely bound to die!'

The trials were to be held at lunch-time. All morning, Karen couldn't concentrate on her lessons. What if she were to miss all her passes? Or worse, an open goal? What if she were to trip herself up?

'Well, Karen?' asked Miss Leader. 'What would happen then?'

'I'd look a right prat!' said Karen, without thinking.

Everyone laughed. Karen jerked herself back to reality.

'So if you multiplied seven by three and took away two, you'd look a right prat, would you?' asked Miss Leader, pointing to the blackboard where she'd written the sum. 'I don't think you've been listening to a word I've been saying!'

'Um . . . er . . . yes I have, you see I wouldn't be able to do the sum, and so I'd look really silly,' said Karen, going red.

'In that case, you obviously need to

practise your tables more,' said Miss Leader. 'I'll give you some extra sums to do at lunch-time.'

Karen sat there, stunned. Lunch-time! She couldn't possibly . . .

'No, we'll make it tonight,' said Miss Leader. 'I shall be busy at lunch-time. You can stay after school for half an hour and do them then.'

'Yes, Miss!' said Karen, smiling all over her face. She'd have willingly stayed for an hour after school, as long as it meant she would be able to take part in the trials at lunch-time.

At last, the bell went. Everyone who wanted was given a chance to try out for the course, so the football field was packed with children kicking balls around. They had to take turns in shooting at goal, taking corners, dribbling round cones, heading, running and passing. Soon, Karen forgot her nerves and just settled down and enjoyed herself doing what she loved best. The ball seemed to run right for her, she didn't do anything terribly wrong, she was quite pleased with herself. Finally, Mr Jay blew the whistle and everyone gathered round, panting and breathless.

'Well, kids!' he said, smiling. 'We've got a lot of young stars in this school. You've all worked hard and I'm really proud of you. But I'm afraid there's only one place on the Football Magic course, so those of you, and that's just about all of you, who aren't picked mustn't feel you've failed. There will be another course next year, I'm sure . . .'

I wish he'd just get on with it, thought Karen, impatiently. All she wanted was to know, one way or the other. Well, there was one other thing she wanted, of course!

'And so, the lucky person is . . . Karen,' said Mr Jay.

Karen stood there, her mouth open. She couldn't believe it. He'd picked her! Hadn't he? Or had she misheard him? Perhaps she'd just been wishing it so much that she'd imagined it? But Dave was smiling at her, someone thumped her on the back and Gary glared at her.

'What?!' she gasped.

'Well done, Kaz,' said Suzie.

'Yeah!' said Dave, grinning. 'You deserve it, I'm really pleased. We'll be relying on you to show them that our school has the best footballers of all.'

* * *

Karen was in a whirl all afternoon. She couldn't wait to get home and tell her mum. She'd be so proud of her, she'd be as excited as she was, or nearly. As the bell rang, Karen was already on her way out of the door when Miss Leader called, 'Karen Tooms! Come and get your detention work!'

Karen couldn't bear it. Long after everyone else had gone, she was sitting at her desk doing the most fiendish multiplications. At last, she'd finished and Miss Leader let her go.

Karen ran all the way home. It's good training for my course, she told herself. From now on, everything in her life would be geared towards going on her course.

'Mum!' she said, bursting through the back door. 'I've done it! I've been picked for Football Magic!'

Her mum dropped the rolling pin. 'You haven't!' she said, going white.

Karen stared at her. There was something wrong. Normally, on hearing such good news, she'd be throwing her rolling pin in the air, squealing with delight and twirling Karen around.

'What?' asked Karen. 'What's wrong?'

'Oh dear,' said her mum. 'I didn't tell you. I didn't think there was any point in worrying you, in case you didn't get the place.'

'Tell me what?' said Karen, quietly, although she had an awful suspicion . . .

'I don't think there's any way we're going to be able to afford it,' said her mum.

CHAPTER 3

They talked about it all weekend.

'I could do a paper round, earn extra money,' said Karen. 'It's my birthday in a fortnight, I could have money from you, and Aunty Jo always sends me ten pounds. I'm sure we could raise the money somehow!'

Her mum sighed. 'Is it really that important, to put everything into going on this course? Once it's over, it's over, and you'll have nothing.'

'Yes, I will!' said Karen. 'I'll have everything I've learnt, it'll make me a much better football player. There will be no question of me not being in the school team any more.'

Her mum smiled. 'Don't you think you earned your place anyway by your performance in the Cup?'

Karen frowned. 'I can't be sure. I feel as though I have to be so much better because I'm a girl. Please, Mum?'

'Eighty pounds,' sighed her mum. 'Well, I suppose if you can raise forty, I'll put in the other half.'

Karen hugged her. 'I will!' she said. 'I've got nearly ten pounds saved up, and then there's my choir money. I'll manage it easily.'

'That's settled then,' said her mum.

'I can tell Mr Jay I can go?'

'You better had,' said her mum. 'Now then, what was that you promised about tidying your room?'

After she'd tidied her room (and found a 50p she didn't know about stuck to a half-finished lolly under her bed), Karen wrote a note:

"Exclusive Baby-sitting Service.
Have your child looked after by someone they know and trust. Just call Karen for any evening: 4 till 10.

Weekends, while you go shopping are a speshillity."

'I'm going to put it through all the doors in the street. What do you think?' asked Karen, showing it to her mum.

'Hmm, change the evening finish to nine, and spell "speciality" right, so they don't think they're employing a brainless wonder, and you may have yourself a nice little job, there,' she said.

'But Mum! Who comes back home at nine o'clock?' protested Karen.

'Lots of people, and you have to get up for your paper round in the morning,' said her mum. 'You'll be so worn out you won't be fit to do anything on this course if you don't watch it!'

On Monday morning, Karen managed to get herself an extra paper round.

'Are you sure you'll have the time to do two rounds before school?' asked Mrs Dawson, at the newsagents.

'Oh, yes!' said Karen. 'I shall run round with them, it will all be good training for my football course.'

Mrs Dawson shook her head.

'Football, indeed! As long as you don't start trying to head the papers through the letter-boxes!'

Karen went to find Mr Jay, as soon as she got to school, but he wasn't in the staff room. At break-time, he was busy coaching basketball, so it wasn't until lunch-time that she was able to tell him the good news.

But he frowned as soon as he saw her.

'Ah, Karen,' he said. 'I'm glad you've come, I was wanting to see you. There's something I've got to tell you.'

'My mum says I can go to Football Magic,' said Karen proudly. 'I hope you don't need the money right away, though. Would the end of term do?'

'Um, well, I'm afraid I've got bad news,' said Mr Jay. 'You see, I wrote to the course organizers on Friday, and told them that you were going to be our school's nominee, and they rang me this morning. It seems . . .'

'What?' asked Karen.

'Well, the thing is, Football Magic isn't open to girls.'

Karen stared at him. She couldn't believe her ears. 'I'm sorry,' she said,

'I don't quite understand . . .'

'It's my fault, I'm afraid,' said Mr Jay. 'I should never have raised your hopes. When all the blurb talked about it being an exciting opportunity for boys, I just thought it said that because they didn't think any girls would be good enough. But it seems that girls just aren't allowed on the course.'

'But that's not fair!' protested Karen.

'I know,' said Mr Jay. 'I'm afraid life isn't always fair.'

Karen stared at him. He wasn't supposed to be sympathizing with her, he was supposed to say that she'd earned her place, he'd make a fuss, write a letter, do anything to make sure she'd get on the course.

'But didn't you tell them that I was the best at the trials?' she said.

'Yes, I told them how brilliant you were, how you loved football as much as any boy, how you scored the winning goal in the Cup, but they wouldn't budge. They said only boys were allowed on the course.'

'But . . . why?' said Karen.

Mr Jay sighed. 'It seems as though they pride themselves on the number of boys who leave their course to go on to play football professionally. They have their photos on the wall to encourage others. One of their boys is now in Leicester City Junior Team reserves.'

'Big deal!' said Karen. 'If I was a boy, I'd be trying for Liverpool first team.'

'I know, Karen,' smiled Mr Jay. 'But the fact remains that you'll never be able to try for any of the big clubs. You'll never be a professional footballer.'

'But what about all the boys who leave the course and go on to be bankers and supermarket shelf-fillers, and maybe just play football on Sundays? I'll be like them, too.'

'I know, Karen. Believe me, I pleaded your case, I told them how disappointed you'd be, but they wouldn't change their minds. They said that once they'd let a girl onto the course, they'd never be able to say no to any others. The floodgates would be open.'

'What a disaster!' said Karen, in mock horror.

Mr Jay smiled, but Karen couldn't. It was as much as she could do to stop herself bursting into tears on the spot.

'I'm sorry,' he said, but she just turned

and walked away, unable to speak.

'Hey, Kaz, come and play football!' called Dave from the other side of the playground. But she just put her head down and walked as fast as she could into the school.

'Kaz! Hey, Kaz!' he yelled, running after her.

She walked in the doors and straight into the girls' toilets. At least he couldn't follow her there. How strange – she'd actually discovered a positive advantage in being a girl!

She went in a cubicle and locked the door behind her. And then she burst into tears. She couldn't believe how unfair life was. How she hated being a girl! It seemed as though boys got the best in everything; they were stronger, taller; they had a lot more fun.

She stayed in the toilets all lunchtime, long after she'd stopped crying. For one thing, her face looked a right mess, and also she knew that if anyone talked to her about the course, she'd burst into tears again. That was another thing about girls, why did they have to cry so much? She couldn't help crying, she hated it, it made her look such a drip, literally! How she wished she was a boy!

As soon as the bell went for afternoon lessons, she emerged and went straight to her desk. Dave came over to her.

'Look, Kaz . . .' he said.

'Don't bother me now, Dave, I'm busy,' she said, turning away.

Dave looked at Suzie, who shrugged and pulled a face, and he went back to his seat.

All afternoon, Karen mechanically got on with her lessons, and then, as soon as the bell went, she flung her books in her bag and dashed out of the classroom.

'Kaz! Kaz, wait!' called Dave, running after her.

Karen walked on faster, but Dave soon caught up with her.

'Talk to me, Kaz, please!' he said. 'I'm sorry, I know you're upset, but it's not my fault.'

Karen stopped. 'You know?' she asked.

Dave nodded. 'I think it's really unfair, it's terrible! You must feel utterly sick!' he said.

Karen nodded, as once more the tears came to her eyes.

'I'd even arranged to do an extra paper round to earn the money,' she said.

'I wanted to go on that course more than anything in the world.'

'I know,' said Dave. 'It's such a marvellous chance. Imagine how I felt when you were picked last week, and I knew that I wouldn't be going. I realize it's not the same, you were the best, you thought you were going to go – you should go!'

Karen looked at him. 'Thanks, Dave,' she said. 'I know I'll get over it, but right now, I just feel so cheated!'

'I know,' said Dave.

'I bet everyone else isn't so sympathetic,' said Karen. 'I bet Gary's laughing his head off!'

'No, he isn't,' said Dave. 'He doesn't know, no-one knows except me. Mr Jay thought it would be better if you got used to the idea that you weren't going, before everyone else started talking about it.'

'Hmm!' said Karen. She started walking again and Dave walked along with her. 'How come you know, then? Did you ask Mr Jay what was the matter with me?'

'No . . .' said Dave slowly.

'What then?' asked Karen. 'How did you find out?' She looked at Dave. He looked odd. She stopped.

'Er, the thing is . . .' he said, not looking at her. Instead, he stared at the ground and started kicking a stone around.

'Yes?'

'Well, he's putting my name forward to go on the course.'

Karen stared at him. She was so angry, she could hardly breathe, let alone talk. There was a pain, tight like a knot across her stomach.

'In my place?' she demanded, finally. 'You're going to take my place on the course?'

'Well, someone has to take it,' Dave said awkwardly.

'I don't believe it!' Karen cried. 'The people who run that course treat me like some . . . some idiot who would be wasting their time, you pretend you're sorry for me, and then the minute they turn round and offer you the place I should have had, you say, "Yes, please, thank you very much!" You can't wait, can you?!'

'Well, it wouldn't help you if I turned the place down, would it?'

'It might have done!' shouted Karen, backing away from him. 'We'll never know now, will we? There's only one thing we do know, and that is, I thought you were my best friend and I was completely wrong. You're worse than my worst enemy!'

And then she ran off, and not surprisingly, Dave didn't follow this time.

CHAPTER 4

Karen's mum was very sympathetic. She listened as Karen told her over and over how unfair life was. She passed her tissues as Karen said how she hated Dave and boys and Mr Jay and everything to do with the stupid football course. When she'd finished, Karen felt a lot better.

'They were probably frightened that you were going to show the boys how much better you were than them!' said her mum. 'After all, not many young footballers have their pictures in the paper.'

'What?' asked Karen.

Her mum passed her the local newspaper. Staring Karen in the face was a picture of herself, holding the Cup, under the heading 'Karen Kicks It In!'

'"The young footballers of Garrett Street Middle School won a marvellous victory over their rivals, Forest Grove, in the final of the Inter-Schools Challenge Cup last week",' said her mum, ' "thanks to a stunning goal in the second half by Karen Tooms. There are those who might think that there is no room for a girl in a football team, but last week Karen proved them well and truly wrong!"'

Karen looked at her mum. She couldn't possibly read the writing from where she was sitting, she must know the words off by heart.

'I'd better send a copy of this to those awful Football Magic people!' said Karen.

'Why stop at one?' said her mum. 'Let's send them a dozen!'

Karen couldn't help but laugh. And then she had an idea.

'Why don't we ring the reporter and tell him what's happened to me? Maybe he'll write about it in the paper? That'll show those course people up. They might even take me after all.'

'Well, I suppose it's worth a try,' said her mum. 'I'll give them a ring now, while the story's "hot", as they say! What's their number?'

She got up and rang the paper, and asked to be put through to the Sports Department. Karen could feel some of the old excitement surging inside her. Maybe, just maybe, she would be going on the course after all? She listened as her mum told the newspaper who she was and explained what had happened. 'She was given the school's place on the course because she was the best footballer in the school,' she said. 'She did best in the trials, she's mad on football, but she's been turned down just because she's a girl! I ask you, is that fair?'

Karen's mum listened to the man on the other end. 'Yes,' she said. 'No . . . I see . . . no . . . right.' And she put the phone down.

'Well?' asked Karen, excitedly.

'They're not interested,' said her mum, glum faced.

'What?!'

'Apparently, it isn't newsworthy enough. And there are no pictures in it.'

'Great!' said Karen. 'I bet if a boy was

36

turned down because he was a boy, it would hit the national papers!'

And then the phone rang.

'Maybe they've changed their minds?' said Karen, rushing to pick it up. But they hadn't. It was Suzie.

'Hi!' she said. 'What was the matter with you this afternoon?'

'Have you got a spare hour?' asked Karen and settled down to tell her.

When Karen went to bed that night, she couldn't sleep. Suddenly there was no focus to her life. First, there had been the Cup to work up to, and then the trials, and then the football course. And now there was nothing. Term was ending soon, the football season was nearly over, there were no more schools' matches, just kicking the ball around in the park with Suzie, Dave and the others.

As she thought about Dave, she felt really guilty. Even though he must have been really disappointed not to be chosen himself, he'd been so pleased for her when she was picked for the course. But when he got her place, she'd been really horrid to him. He'd done really well to be second choice for the course, and it wasn't his fault she wasn't going. Being nasty to Dave hadn't made her feel any better at all, in fact, it had made her feel a lot worse.

As it turned out, Dave was the first person she saw on her way to school the next day. He was on the other side of the road, but he didn't cross over to walk with her, like he normally did. He even pretended he hadn't seen her. She couldn't blame him. She ran across to him.

'I'm sorry, Dave,' she said.

He stopped and looked at her and pulled a face. 'I'm sorry, too. You really ought to be going on the course. Somehow I can't get as excited about it as I would have been.'

'Oh, you mustn't be like that,' said Karen. 'You must go and enjoy it, get everything out of it. If anyone had to go in my place, I'm glad it's you. Maybe when you come back, you can pass on a few tips to me?'

Dave smiled at her. 'Sure thing!' he said. 'I could ring you each night, tell you what I've learnt, and if there are any questions you want me to ask, I'll pass them on.'

'Great!' said Karen. 'Look, I'd worked out a training plan, to get me ready for the course. Perhaps we could do it together?'

'Brilliant!' said Dave. 'Hey, I liked your photo in the paper. I bet you were proud!'

'A bit!' said Karen, blushing. 'My mum's bought six copies to send to all my aunts and uncles. Talk about embarrassing!'

'My mum's told everyone I've been picked for the course,' said Dave. 'We're going out shopping on Saturday to buy me a new tracksuit and football boots.'

'New boots!' gasped Karen. Her boots were tatty and worn and they rubbed her toes. She'd been admiring Dave's boots for weeks, he'd only had them since Christmas!

'Well, I've nearly grown out of my old ones. Tell you what,' said Dave, 'you can have them, if you like, they're probably your size. Have my old tracksuit, too, it'll only go to some jumble sale.'

'Great!' said Karen, smiling at him. Maybe boys weren't so awful after all? Well, not all of them, anyway.

CHAPTER 5

It was half-way through the first week of the holiday that it happened. Karen and Dave had been practising shooting at an imaginary goal in the park, and afterwards they went to play on the climbing frame. Karen was a better gymnast than Dave, but he was always more daring. Now he was swinging upside down from the highest bar.

'Hold on tight, Dave!' called Karen, feeling a bit like her mum must do, when she shouted at Karen not to lean too far out of the bedroom window.

'I'm OK!' said Dave. And then he let go with one hand, and then the other, just holding on by the backs of his knees.

Karen could hardly breathe. It was over two metres to the ground. She watched as he leaned back up to grab hold of the bar, and she heaved a sigh of relief. And then it happened so quickly, Karen wasn't quite sure how. Somehow, Dave slipped and without even a cry he fell to the ground in a heap. Karen stared in horror as he just lay there, quietly, not moving at all.

'Dave! Dave!' she called, running up to him. For one awful moment she thought he must have died, but then she realized that he was breathing, quite heavily.

'Dave! Where are you hurt? Speak to me!' cried Karen desperately, not daring to touch him. But Dave just lay there. Then he moved his head to one side and groaned. Karen noticed that one of his legs was at a strange angle beneath him – he must have broken it. But what else might he have broken? His face was an awful grey-white colour. She must do something, quickly. She looked around her, but the park, which had been crowded with little children and their mothers only a few moments before, was strangely deserted. She'd never felt more alone in her life. What was she to do?

'I'll be back in a minute, Dave!' she cried. 'Don't worry, you'll be all right.' She wasn't sure if he could hear her, but it made her feel a lot better to say it. She got up and ran to the main road as fast as she could and waved at the cars that were driving past. Some of them carried on, as though she was just a silly child having fun, but finally one of them stopped, and the man wound down his window.

'Help me, please!' begged Karen. 'My friend's had an accident in the park. It's very serious!'

Even as she was speaking, the man had picked up his mobile phone and was ringing for an ambulance. Then he dialled Karen's mum's number for her. He handed the phone to Karen.

'Mum!' she cried. 'There's been an accident at the park – Dave's hurt. The ambulance is coming.'

'What?' said her mum. 'Is he all right?'

'I don't know,' said Karen. 'Oh Mum, come quick!'

Within two minutes, Karen's mum was racing across the field. Karen had never seen her run so fast. Later, it occurred to her that that must be where she got her fast running speed from, but she couldn't think about that then. All she could think was how scared she was, and how pleased she was to see her mum. Poor Dave still hadn't opened his eyes. He looked paler than ever.

'Right,' said her mum, loosening his shirt at the neck, and then feeling for a pulse. 'He's breathing, that's good. What happened?'

Karen told her, and how the man had come to their aid, and promised to stay until the ambulance arrived.

'Thank you,' said her mum, smiling at him. 'Dave's certainly got a broken leg and concussion, maybe he's injured his back too. That's why we mustn't move him. But he's young and fit, I'm sure he'll be all right. Good, here's the ambulance!'

Karen was amazed at how cool, calm and collected her mum was. Normally, she went into a flap at the slightest thing, but it seemed that here she knew just what to do. She got up and talked to the ambulanceman, and Karen watched as they carefully lifted Dave into the ambulance. He made the most awful groaning noise, and Karen shuddered.

'Now, love, you go on home and I'll go

with Dave to the hospital,' said her mum.

'Oh, Mum!' moaned Karen. 'I'm so worried, I have to be there with him! Please let me come, too?'

'Oh, all right,' said her mum. 'Come on, get in, quick then!'

Karen had always wanted to ride in an ambulance with its siren blazing and lights flashing, but now she wished with all her heart that she was back in the park, playing with Dave. But in no time at all, they were at the hospital and Dave was being wheeled into a cubicle, while Karen and her mum were told to sit and wait in the waiting area. Karen's mum went off to try to contact Dave's mum, but she was out, so she just left a message at her office.

Then the doctor came in and took Karen's mum off to one side, and she signed some papers. She was smiling as she walked back to Karen.

'Dave's regained consciousness,' she told her, 'and they think his leg is the only problem. They're taking him off for an X-ray, now, to check.'

Karen couldn't help but worry. What if it wasn't just his leg, what if he'd damaged his spine? What if he was going to be in a wheelchair for the rest of his life? She should have stopped him swinging on that bar, he was only doing it to impress her, it was all her fault.

'If you bite those nails any more, you won't have any fingers left!' said her mum.

Karen frowned.

'If you're missing your lunch, why don't you go and get a Mars bar or something?' suggested her mum.

Karen shook her head. She couldn't eat a thing. She watched the clock, it seemed to take forever for the minutes to go by. Then Dave's mum arrived in a right state, but Karen's mum soothed her and told her all would be well. Karen could hardly look at her, sure that she would blame Karen for letting her son nearly kill himself.

'Karen acted very quickly and sensibly,' said her mum. 'Thanks to her, Dave was in hospital within five minutes.'

Dave's mum turned to her.

'Thank you, Karen,' she said, tearfully, squeezing her hand.

And then the doctor came rushing

back in, his white coat flaring out behind him.

'Mrs Burrows? Hello, I've got good news. As we thought, your son's leg is broken, just below the knee, but that's all. He had mild concussion, but he's fully conscious now. We've given him an injection to stop the pain, and then we're going to set and plaster his leg. Would you like to see him first?'

'Oh, yes please, thank you!' said Mrs Burrows, bustling after the doctor.

Karen smiled at her mum. Suddenly, she was absolutely starving.

After his leg had been plastered and his mum had left, Karen and her mum were allowed to see Dave. Karen was relieved to see that his cheeks were now almost back to their usual rosy colour, and he smiled up at her.

'You had me really worried, there,' she told him. 'Next time you want to break your neck, make sure you do it while I'm not around!'

Dave grinned.

'Will you be the first to sign my plaster?' he asked her.

'What? "Ding-bat"? "Air-head"? Or

would you prefer "Prize Idiot"?' asked Karen, taking a pen from her mum. She thought for a moment and then grinned and wrote:

Dave swung so high
He thought he could fly,
But he very soon found,
That he'd flown to the ground.
Happy Landings,
Kaz.

'I'm glad you're all right, now, Dave,' said Karen's mum. 'I've never seen Karen so upset in my life, not even when she was turned down for that football course.'

Karen gasped and stared at Dave. She'd been so worried, it hadn't occurred to her before.

'Oh no!' she exclaimed. 'Football Magic! You'll have to miss it! What are we going to do?'

CHAPTER 6

Karen's mum knew exactly what to do.

'You'll just have to ring Mr Jay and tell him what's happened. He'll contact his next choice for the course and check they can go before notifying Manchester. You can ring him as soon as we get home, Karen.'

Karen frowned. 'What if that person can't go?' she asked.

'Someone will be able to. From what you said, the whole school wanted to go to Football Magic.'

'Um, I suppose so,' said Karen. She turned back to Dave. 'I'm really sorry, Dave. Tough luck!'

'We're both in the same boat, now,' he said, ruefully. 'We both thought we were going and now we can't. That course seems fated.'

'Right!' said a nurse, walking into the cubicle. 'It's time to take Dave up to his ward. You two can come and visit him tonight between seven and nine.'

'Get my mum to bring in my football mags, will you?' asked Dave. 'And my Game Boy.'

'Right,' said Karen. 'And I'll let you know who's going on the course.'

When she went back to visit Dave that night, Karen had a strange smile on her face. Dave's leg was suspended in the air by a collection of ropes; he looked really silly, as though he was trying to walk towards the ceiling, but that wasn't why she was smiling.

'How are you feeling?' she asked.

'My head hurts where I banged it when I fell, and now the anaesthetic's worn off, my leg is really throbbing,' said Dave.

'Same as usual, then!' said Karen, grinning.

'I knew I'd get a load of sympathy off you!' said Dave. 'What's that silly smile for, anyway?'

'What?' asked Karen, innocently. But she couldn't keep her face straight.

'Come on!' said Dave. 'You're dying to tell me, anyway.'

'It's about Football Magic,' said Karen.

'Oh!' groaned Dave. 'I don't know how you can think about that and smile at the same time. I can't! So come on, tell me, who's going in my place?'

'Me,' said Karen.

'What?' Dave was so surprised, he jerked his leg in its sling. 'Ow!' he yelled. 'Aaah! Don't do that to me! Ooooh! Any movement is agony!'

'Sorry,' said Karen.

'Just don't make me move it again!' said Dave slowly, his eyes closed. 'No surprises, OK?'

'OK,' said Karen. 'I'm really sorry.'

'So, tell me,' said Dave, when he'd finally got himself comfortable once more. 'How come the Football Magic people have changed their minds and allowed a girl on their course? I can't believe it!'

'They haven't,' said Karen.

Dave groaned. 'My head aches, I'm not up to riddles, just tell me, OK?'

'Right,' said Karen. 'Well, when I got home, I rang Mr Jay, like my mum said, but there was no answer. I rang him again two hours later, but still no reply, so Mum suggested that I went round to his house and put a note through his door, to tell him what had happened, to make sure he could contact someone straight away. So I did, but I rang the bell first, to check if he was in, and this old lady from next door came out to see what was happening. And then she told me that Mr Jay has gone away on a camping holiday somewhere in Scotland and won't be back until after Easter.'

'Lucky him!' said Dave.

'So, on the way home, I thought about it. No-one but Mr Jay knows who is the next best football player at our school, do they?'

'Well, I do, but . . .'

'No-one official, I mean,' said Karen. 'None of the teachers. So no-one can say who should go on the course. You and I know who we'd pick . . .'

'Steve,' said Dave.

'Maybe, but we can't ring Steve and

tell him he's going on the course, can we? It's not up to us.'

'No,' said Dave.

'So, no-one can go on the course, can they?'

'But that's not fair,' said Dave. 'We ought to use the place we've been given.'

'Quite,' said Karen. 'After all, if we don't bother to send someone this year, they might not even give us a place next year.'

'That's true,' said Dave. 'But they won't let you go, they've already said that.'

'They won't if they know it's me,' said Karen. 'But if I go as you . . . ?'

'No!' said Dave. 'Ow!! Aaaah!' He closed his eyes in agony. 'You've made me do it again!' he whispered.

'I'm sorry, but it's your fault, you mustn't over-react!' said Karen. 'Just calm down and think about it. No-one knows what you look like. I could cut my hair – I don't look that much like a girl. I'm sure I could pass as a boy.'

'No!' said Dave.

'What difference would it make to you? Either I go or no-one goes, and I was the first one to earn a place on the course anyway! I should go! I could pass on all the tips to you, like you were going to do to me. You've got nothing to lose, I'll be the one taking all the risks of being found out.'

'You will be found out,' said Dave. 'Definitely.'

'I don't think so. They won't be expecting a girl, I don't play football like a girl, and that's what they'll all be looking at, mostly. It'll be easy.'

'It won't work,' said Dave. 'And when they find out, there'll be the most almighty row!'

'I'll run that risk,' said Karen. 'You can say you didn't know anything about my plan. After all, you're stuck in hospital, you couldn't stop me even if you wanted to!'

'I could tell your mum!' said Dave. 'She's walking down the ward right now.'

'Don't!' begged Karen. 'Please, Dave!'

Dave looked at her and shook his head.

'Please?!' she pleaded.

'Hello, there! I've bought you some chocolates, Dave!' said Karen's mum, sitting down on the other chair by the bed. 'According to Karen, these are your

53

favourites. I wanted her to come with me to help choose but she was so desperate to come and see you straight away.'

'Thank you, Mrs Tooms,' said Dave, his eyes lighting up. 'They are my favourite!'

'Good. How are you?'

'Oh, I'm fine . . . except when I'm made to move my leg,' he said, glaring at Karen.

'So what was it?' asked Mrs Tooms.

'What?'

'The news Karen was so desperate to tell you. Who is going to go to Football Magic? She wouldn't tell me, she said she had to tell you first, but by the smile on her face when she came back from seeing Mr Jay, it's obviously someone she approves of.'

Dave opened his mouth and looked at Karen. She shot a pleading look at him. He closed it again.

'I'm going!' said Karen, before he could say anything to the contrary.

'What?!' exclaimed her mum, so loudly that several other patients and their visitors turned and looked.

Karen beamed at her, nodding her head.

'I can't believe it!' cried her mum, getting up. 'How fantastic! How wonderful! Oh, I really can't believe it! They were so set against you before! What on earth made them change their minds?'

'Shh, Mum! People are looking,' whispered Karen.

'Oh,' said her mum, looking around and sitting down again. Then she leaned forward eagerly. 'Well, this is a turn up for the books. Women's Lib strikes again, eh? Isn't it amazing, Dave?'

'Totally unbelievable!' muttered Dave.

'Oh Karen, I'm so pleased for you, darling,' said her mum, hugging her.

'Thanks,' said Karen. Dave glared at her over her mum's shoulder.

'Aren't you pleased for her, Dave?' asked her mum.

'I'm dumbstruck!' said Dave, trying to be sarcastic.

'Of course, it's really tragic that you aren't going,' said Karen's mum. 'But if you can't go, at least Karen gets another chance. I'm sure she'll tell you all about it!'

'Oh, I'm sure she will!' said Dave. 'I can't wait to hear what happens.'

Karen's mum could tell, even through

her excitement, that something was wrong.

'Is your leg hurting, Dave?' she asked.

'I'm suffering from a bit of a pain!' said Dave, looking pointedly at Karen.

'Maybe we shouldn't stay too long,' said Karen's mum. 'After all, your mum's coming at eight. Is there anything you'd like Karen to bring you tomorrow?'

'You could borrow my personal stereo, if you like,' suggested Karen. 'And any tapes you want. They might just stop you worrying too much.'

'Worrying?' said Karen's mum. 'His leg's been set, all he's got to do is lie back and wait for it to heal. He's in the best place. What's Dave got to worry about?'

'Nothing,' said Karen. 'That's what I was telling him. I'll see you tomorrow, Dave, right? There's afternoon visiting, I'll come on my own.'

'Thanks,' said Dave. 'Thanks a million. I can't wait!'

CHAPTER 7

'Well?' said Karen, the next afternoon. 'Got used to the idea, yet?'

'No,' said Dave. 'The more I think about it, the more sure I am that it isn't going to work. And wearing that silly hat on your head isn't going to make me feel any better about it.'

Karen grinned, and took it off, to reveal her new hair-style.

'You've cut your hair!' gasped Dave, only just managing not to move his leg. 'I told you not to give me any nasty shocks!'

'I said I was going to cut it,' said Karen. 'The course starts on Monday, I've got to start getting ready.'

'What on earth did your mum say?' he asked.

'She hasn't seen it, yet,' said Karen, pulling a face. 'Well, what do you think of it? What do I look like?'

'A girl,' said Dave.

'That's because you know I'm a girl. If you didn't, you could easily think I was a boy.'

'Yeah, if I was half blind. Or my brain had stopped working. But, unfortunately for you, it was only my leg I hurt yesterday.'

'I do look like a boy!' said Karen. 'Thank goodness my mum wouldn't let me have my ears pierced. I never thought I'd be grateful for that!'

'It takes more than ears without holes to look like a boy,' said Dave.

'We'll see!' said Karen. 'Watch this! Excuse me, !' she called to a passing nurse.

'Yes?'

'I bet you can't guess what my name is.'

'Um, Cathy? Sharon? Linda?'

'No, never mind,' said Karen, pulling a face.

'See!' laughed Dave, 'She thinks you're

a girl!' He rolled about the bed. 'Ow! Ow! My leg!'

'It's only because I was wearing pink trousers and a purple top,' said Karen. 'If I was wearing jeans and a Wrestling Fed top, just like yours, they'd be convinced I was a boy.'

'No!' said Dave, 'you're not borrowing my wrestling top.'

'Well, if you want me to be found out, if you want everyone to think Dave Burrows walks round in wimpish girlie clothes . . .'

'I don't . . .' began Dave. He stopped and frowned. Then he heaved a big sigh. 'You're going to go through with it, whatever I say, aren't you?'

'Yes,' smiled Karen.

'What if I have to play football with any of these boys in the future?'

'You won't! They're from all over the county, even if you should ever meet them again, you'll just have to say I'm your cousin or something.'

'More lies,' said Dave. 'You lied to your mum . . .'

'I didn't! I was very careful not to! I just said I was going on the course — she assumed all the rest about them changing their minds. If you like, you can always say it must be some other Dave Burrows, after all, that's true, the name's not all that unusual. I'll call myself David to be a bit different.'

'You're really keen to go through with it, aren't you?' said Dave.

'Desperate!' said Karen. 'I'll pass on all the tips to you!'

'Oh, all right,' said Dave, reluctantly. 'I'll help you. I haven't got any choice, really. I'm stuck here, tied to the bed, and I know you'll only pester me until I agree. As long as you say I knew nothing of it, if it goes wrong.'

'Agreed!' said Karen, bouncing up and down.

'And as long as you stop bouncing on my bed!'

'Oh, right, sorry,' said Karen, moving to the chair. 'I was just so excited. Thanks, Dave, you won't regret it. Look,' she said, feeling in her pocket and handing him a piece of paper. 'I've got a list of all the things I'd like to borrow from you. Can I still have your old football boots?'

'Yeah!' said Dave, unfolding the list.

'Oh, and don't over-react!' added

Karen quickly. But she was too late.

'No!' exclaimed Dave.

'Dave! I have to! We're going to have to get changed together, aren't we?'

'But my boxer shorts! You can't get more personal than that, Kaz!'

'If I could afford to buy my own, I would,' said Karen. 'Please, Dave?'

Yet again, Dave, unable to move, lying with his foot stuck stupidly in the air, knew when he was beaten.

'Look,' he said, 'I tell you what, you call round to my house tonight and tell my mum you're getting some things for me, and then just help yourself to whatever you need, OK? Only don't tell me what you take, I don't want to know, just make sure it's all back, clean and in one piece, when I get out of hospital.'

'Oh thanks, Dave!' said Karen, flinging herself at him. Only just in time, she remembered his leg.

'You should walk round with a DANGER sign slung round your neck,' protested Dave. 'Get back off the bed!'

'OK!' said Karen. 'I think you're brilliant!'

'Just make sure you don't get found

out!' said Dave. 'I'm relying on you, Kaz!'

'I won't!' she said. 'Oh, Dave, you're magic, you won't regret it! I promise.'

'Hmm!' said Dave.

'By the way, how are you feeling today?' she asked.

'Oh, thanks for asking! What wonderful concern you show!' said Dave, sarcastically. 'Actually, I was feeling all right until you came in.'

'You're a fraud!' said Karen. 'Here, have some football mags!'

On the way out, Karen stopped a porter.

'Excuse me, my name's Gary Peters, I'm looking for my mum on ward twelve,' she said.

'Oh, right, you go along the corridor and turn right and it's facing you, Gary,' said the porter.

'Thanks!' said Karen. The porter looked after her in amazement as she walked off in completely the opposite direction. He was even more surprised when she leapt in the air and yelled 'Hooray!'

'What?!' exclaimed Karen's mum, in horror, when she walked in. 'Who are you? What's happened to my precious daughter?'

'Oh, Mum!' said Karen. 'I've only cut my hair.'

'*Cut* it!' cried her mum. 'There's hardly any left!'

'Well,' said Karen, 'it'll grow again.'

'But why?' wailed her mum. 'I'd just about got used to a daughter who preferred chasing a ball around a muddy pitch rather than bake cakes with me, I'd even got used to not being able to tie ribbons in your hair, but to have a daughter who looks more like a boy . . .'

'What?' asked Karen, her eyes shining.

'You. You look more like a boy than a girl!'

'Oh, Mum!' Karen cried and hugged her.

Her mum pulled back suspiciously. 'Is this what this is all about? You want to look like a boy? It's not on, Karen, you're a girl, you must accept that, and be proud of it.'

'Oh, I do!' said Karen. 'I do, really. I just thought, well, it might help me fit in on the course next week if I looked more like a boy. I wouldn't stick out so much.'

'But you should be proud that you're a girl and that you've won a place all on your own merits, despite that.'

'I am,' said Karen. 'But I don't want anyone treating me any differently because I'm a girl. I don't want any favours on the pitch. Or to be left out. That happens a lot in the school team, especially with boys like Gary. But from a distance, with my hair like this, hopefully the others might forget that I'm not the same as them and pass the ball to me. That's all that matters.'

Her mum looked at her. 'It may not be easy, being the only girl there. You aren't having second thoughts, are you?'

'Oh no!' said Karen. 'I can't wait! In fact, I think I'll go and start getting my things together now.'

'So you're off, then?' said Dave, three days later.

'Yes,' said Karen. 'Sorry I won't be able to visit you for a week.'

Dave pulled a face. 'I'll survive.'

'You can ring me at the college after eight, if you like. Here's the number. I'll fill you in on everything.'

'Right,' said Dave, taking the bit of paper from her.

'Only don't ask for Karen Tooms!' she warned him. 'Or say it's Dave Burrows calling.'

'I won't!' said Dave. 'What's your mum going to do?'

'I said we can't have incoming calls. I'll have to ring her every night.'

'It's going to go wrong, you know, don't you?' said Dave.

'It won't. And even if it does, what will they do? Send me home in disgrace? At least I'll have had part of the course, which is more than I would have had.'

'They'll find out on the first day. What about having showers and that?'

'I'll say I've got athlete's foot. I've got it all worked out, Dave.'

'What if you have to share a room?'

'I'll deal with that if I have to.'

'Hmm.' Dave didn't look convinced. 'Steve came in today. He was asking what was happening about Football Magic.'

'What did you tell him?'

'That my place had been filled by someone else.'

'Good,' said Karen.

'He asked who it was.'

'Oh. What did you say?'

'I pretended my leg had suddenly started to hurt and sent him off to get me a drink of fresh water. Then, when he came back, I showed him all my football mags and he forgot about his question.'

'Nice one,' smiled Karen. 'Here, I brought you some more choccies. You'll be so fat when you come out of here, you won't fit into any of your clothes.'

'If I've got any left,' moaned Dave. 'Have you taken everything you need from my room?'

'Yes,' said Karen. 'Your mum looked at me a bit oddly when I came out with a holdall stuffed full of things, so I said you'd asked for your school books.'

'She'd have looked at you even more oddly, after that!' exclaimed Dave.

'Well, it was all I could think of on the spur of the moment. As long as she doesn't go looking in your drawers, you'll be all right. And I gave her the eighty pounds back that she'd paid for the course. She said she was going to buy you something nice with it.'

'Did she?' said Dave, his eyes lighting up.

'Well, I suggested it, actually.'

'You did! Fantastic!' Dave cried, excitedly. 'Tell her I want a portable hand-held TV!'

'I did,' smiled Karen. 'I even pointed out to her the one you were drooling over in the catalogue.'

'Oh, Kaz, you're brilliant!' said Dave. 'You don't know what it's like here, everyone else wants to watch *Emmerdale* and *Countdown*!'

'You've told me, twenty-million times. And I told your mum!' said Karen. 'I think she might be bringing it in tonight!'

'That was really wicked of you,' said Dave. 'Thanks a million.'

'Well, one good turn deserves another,' said Karen.

'Yeah!' smiled Dave.

'I'd better go,' said Karen. 'I promised my mum I wouldn't be late, last night at home, and everything.'

'OK,' said Dave. 'Good luck on the course, with the football, too.'

'Thanks!' said Karen, getting up. She turned to go.

'Oh, and Kaz?'

'Yes?' She looked back at Dave.

'You look just like a boy!' he said.

Karen grinned and gave him the thumbs up sign. Then she turned and sauntered down the ward, just the way a boy would. Or so she thought.

CHAPTER 8

Karen's mum wanted to go on the coach with her all the way to the Football Magic Training Centre, and was very upset when Karen insisted that she wanted to go on her own. She even tried to change her daughter's mind as they stood waiting for the coach.

'But, Mum! I'll look such a sissy!' said Karen. 'You can wait with me until I get on the coach, but after that, I'll be on my own. After all, the coach stops right outside the college, and it will save money if you don't come, too.'

'You seem so independent now,' said her mum. 'You wouldn't even let me help you pack!'

Karen frowned. And let her see Dave's boxer shorts? Not likely!

'I'm growing up, Mum. I'm not your little baby girl any more.'

'You're not even my girl any more!' said her mum. 'You're more like my boy! Since when did you start to like wrestling? I never thought I'd see you going round with that logo on your front. You used to say it was stupid!'

'I'm more tolerant, now,' said Karen. 'Look, there's the coach! Now, Mum . . .'

'What?'

'Promise me you're not going to cry, here, in front of everyone.'

'I'm not!' said her mum, firmly. 'Take care, darling, and make sure you don't let those boys tease you. Show them you're as good as they are.'

'Oh, I won't do that!' said Karen. 'I'll show them I'm even better!'

Karen felt very alone when she stepped off the coach. Clutching her bags, she wandered up the long driveway to the course headquarters, a desolate-looking brick building surrounded by massive areas of playing fields. Just outside, she met a boy hanging around. He had fair hair and freckles and he looked very big.

'Hi,' he said. 'Are you on Football Magic?'

'Yes,' said Karen.

'Great, I was hoping someone else would arrive soon. I'm Andy!'

'Hello, I'm David Burrows,' said Karen. She waited for him to laugh, and say 'You're not a boy!', but he didn't. He said something worse.

'You're in the same room as me!'

Karen stared at him in horror, but he didn't seem to notice.

'Brilliant!' he said, opening a door. 'You just have to go in here and sign the book and then I'll show you where everything is.'

Karen groaned inwardly. She'd been so sure she'd have a room of her own! She followed Andy up the stairs and along endless white-painted, drab corridors, lugging her bags. She had hoped he'd offer to carry one for her, but he didn't. But then, he thought she was a boy, didn't he?

Finally, he stopped and flung open a door. 'Here we are!' he said. 'It's not exactly a palace, but I'm sure we'll have fun.'

'But . . . it's got four beds!' exclaimed Karen, looking around her in horror.

'Yes. Paul and Leroy are in here, too. They've gone out to practise already.'

'Oh . . .'

'They're really nice!' said Andy, noting the look on her face.

'Oh, yes, I'm sure they are,' said Karen. 'I just didn't think it was going to be this crowded.'

'Look, why don't we go and join them?' said Andy. 'Our first session isn't until after lunch, but what's the point in hanging around?'

'OK,' said Karen.

He stood there, waiting. She looked at him, uncertainly. And then it dawned on her, he was going to stay and watch her get changed!

'Um, look, I'll just unpack first if you don't mind,' said Karen, awkwardly. 'You go on!'

'All right,' he said. 'We're out there, look, you can see the pitch through that window.'

He left her, and Karen gazed out of the window at the other boys practising. They all seemed to have made friends already, as though being away from home didn't bother them. And they looked so much bigger than her. They were sure to be better than her. She should never have come!

She gazed around the room. Its cream paint was cracked and peeling in one corner, the floor was covered in an awful faded brown carpet, and there was a single heavy oak dressing table with a mirror on it, blocking the window. The only other furniture was the beds, each covered with a gaudy orange bedspread, each with a cupboard next to it.

There was one that had nothing strewn over it, so she assumed that was hers. At least it was tucked away in the corner. She went over and put all her clothes in the cupboard next to it and then slid her empty bags underneath. How she wished she'd been able to bring Matty! She'd spent every night with her cuddly monkey for as long as she could remember. She'd even thought of keeping him secretly zipped up in her bag, for she didn't suppose that boys took cuddly toys to bed with them. But in the end, she'd left him at home. After all, to be caught with Matty would ruin everything.

She sat on a chair, thought of her mum and felt very alone. There was a pain in her tummy, dull and aching, like a great big hole. She'd got almost a whole week here, five long days and nights that seemed to stretch ahead of her, endlessly. How could she possibly endure it? It would have been so easy to fling herself down on her bed and cry her eyes out . . . Instead, she stood up quickly and forced herself to get changed. Then she ran out to the field. Andy was dribbling around some cones, then he dodged a tackle from another boy and shot at the goal. He was brilliant!

'Yes!' he cried. He ran and picked up the ball from the back of the net, turned and saw Karen.

'Hi!' he called. 'What took you so long? Here!' He threw the ball at her. 'We'll play against each other!'

As soon as she started kicking the ball around, Karen felt better. OK, Andy was good, but she could still manage to get the ball round him. After about ten minutes, they stopped, and got together with the others. Andy introduced her. There was Kev and Mitch and Greg as well as Leroy and Paul.

'Hey! You're tiny,' said Leroy, looking down on her. 'What do they call you? Titch?'

Karen shook her head. 'David.'

'You David, me Goliath!' laughed Leroy. 'What's your best footballing skill, David?'

'Well, I don't know . . . I can run a bit . . .'

'Run a bit! Is that all? I'm brilliant at scoring goals!' said Paul.

'Not as good as me!' said Kev. 'And you should see the way I tackle! I hope you've all brought shin pads!'

'I'll be able to get past you easy!' said Andy. 'I'm brilliant at everything.'

'Same here!' said Mitch. 'I'm captain of our school team. I was in it when I was in the second year! My dad's going to arrange for me to have a try-out with Watford as soon as I'm old enough.'

'Watford!' exclaimed Greg. 'That second-rate club! I'm going to play for Arsenal one day.'

'Spurs is the club for me,' said Leroy. 'They need someone to head a few goals in for them. I wonder if I should offer myself now, instead of waiting till I'm sixteen?'

Everyone laughed.

'I shouldn't bother!' said Andy.

'No,' said Leroy. 'Not the state they're in – they wouldn't be able to afford me!'

'Ha! Ha!' said Kev, as the others giggled.

'You know, it's difficult trying to choose my best skill, because I'm such an all-rounder, but I reckon heading comes top,' continued Leroy. 'My long legs get me around like a tornado, but when I'm in the box, I just tower over everyone. All I have to do is stand and wait for the ball. How on earth do you manage to head the ball, David?'

'I jump!' said Karen, defensively.

'Well, I suppose you must be able to, if you've won a place on this course, unless you're all midgets where you come from. Where's that anyway?'

'Garrett Street Middle School,' she said, proudly.

'Hey, that's near us. Didn't you win the Inter-Schools Cup?' asked Kev. 'There was something in the paper. Don't you have a girl in your team?'

'Er, yeah,' said Karen.

'The team won the Cup and they went and put just her picture in the paper!'

Kev told the others. 'Just because she's a girl, I ask you!'

'She did score the winning goal,' said Karen, indignantly.

'It was a team effort, though, wasn't it?' demanded Kev. 'I mean, someone had to pass her the ball, and stop the goals at the other end. She wasn't the only person playing, I take it?'

Karen glared at him. No-one said that when Alan Shearer's photo was plastered all over the back pages when he scored the winning goal for England.

'Hey, Titch, that girl in the paper looked rather like you,' said Kev. 'Come to think of it, she was almost the spitting image. Wait . . . I think I know why you're standing up for her!'

Karen stared at him, miserably. To be found out so soon!

'She's your sister, isn't she?' he said. 'Probably your twin.'

Karen smiled. 'You guessed!' she said. 'But I tell you this, she might be a girl, but she's still good at football.'

'You're not the slightest bit biased, of course, are you, Titch?' said Kev, grinning at her.

She glared back at him and hoped all

the boys weren't going to be like Kevin.

'Come on!' said Paul. 'Let's play some more football. We'll divide into teams, Andy and I will be captains.'

Each of them picked their team, three in each side until there was one person left. Karen. No-one wanted her – they could tell she was useless. She felt so miserable, she just wanted to sink into the ground.

Paul looked at her. 'Titch can go with Andy,' he said. 'We're going to beat his team anyway.'

Karen smarted. They all thought they were so good! Well, she'd show them. They lined up on the pitch, and then Leroy started off with the ball. Karen ran towards him, and he continued to come at her, Leroy with his long legs and fast run. He kicked the ball ahead of him, taunting her, and Karen ran for it. She just managed to get a foot there first. Leroy tried to tackle her, but she turned and twisted, and with his great big body, he just couldn't keep up with her.

She headed towards the goal. Kevin bore down on her, large and intimidating. Karen recalled what he'd said about how he tackled, so she kicked the ball to one side and darted after it, leaving him behind. Now there was just Paul left between her and the goal. On her right, Andy was yelling for the ball, but she ignored him. She had to show them. She paused, flicked the ball onto her right foot, took a deep breath, and shot. As she watched the ball go sailing into the back of the net, it was the sweetest moment of her life, far sweeter than when she'd scored in the Inter-Schools Cup Final.

'Hey, you're not bad!' said Andy. 'Why didn't you tell us how good you were?'

Karen smiled to herself. He'd seen nothing yet!

CHAPTER 9

As they walked back in to have lunch, after a brilliant game into which Karen had put every ounce of effort, no-one called her 'Titch' any more. She felt good; after her disastrous start, she knew it was going to be all right after all.

'You must give me some tips on avoiding tackles,' said Andy. 'You're so nifty, you're almost like a ballet dancer!'

Karen smiled. For the first time ever, she was grateful to her mum for forcing her to go to ballet lessons when she was five.

'Your tackling's pretty good,' she told him.

'Well, it needs to be with all the talent around here!' said Andy.

When they got inside, the other course members were waiting, all thirty-seven of them! They were standing around in a big, noisy group.

'We'll stick together on this course, shall we?' she whispered to Andy. 'I feel a bit lost amongst all this lot.'

'Don't mind, if you want,' said Andy with a shrug.

Karen smiled with relief. He might not mind, but she did. She needed to feel there was going to be at least one friendly face in the crowd. Why was everyone so full of confidence, apart from her?

After lunch, the course started properly. They were put in small groups, and worked with coaches on individual skills. Karen and Andy were together. It was hard work. It seemed as though whatever they did was wrong. All Brian, the chief coach, seemed to do, was point out their mistakes.

'Stretch for the ball, David!' he commanded. 'Run faster! Come on, you haven't got lead weights in your boots!'

Karen felt as though she had.

Whatever she did, Brian wanted more: more press-ups, more balls on target, more speed on the turn, more headers reached. Fortunately, he was the same with everyone.

'No-one said it was going to be living torture, here!' said Andy, when they paused for a drink. 'I thought this course was supposed to be fun!'

'Come on!' yelled Brian. 'Back to work, we'll have a match now, that is, if any of you can remember what the goal's for!'

The match was brilliant fun. When Karen scored, there were no sarky comments about hogging the ball because she was a girl, there was no-one who wouldn't pass the ball to her because she was different. When the game was finally over, she felt elated but totally shattered.

They all went into the changing room, to have their showers.

'Come on, David, don't just stand there!' yelled Brian. 'Dinner's in half an hour.'

'Um, I can't have a shower, I've got athlete's foot,' she said.

'Have you got a doctor's note?'

'Er . . . no . . .'

'Well, then, you can have a shower!'

'Couldn't I have a bath instead?' she pleaded. 'I could leave my foot dangling out so I don't infect the bath?'

'Oh, go on, then! But make sure you're quick!'

Karen heaved a sigh of relief and dashed upstairs. It was going to be all right.

She was a bit late for dinner, but Andy had saved her a place. Everyone talked about rollerblading and their BMXs and wrestling and judo and boasted about how good they were. It was as though they all had to prove themselves, like they had at the beginning on the football pitch. Even Andy bragged about his new skateboard and how fast he could go. What did it matter? They were here to play football, weren't they?

After dinner, they were given a talk about tactics and watched a video of a professional football match. After five minutes, Brian stopped the tape.

'Now then,' he said, 'what do you think the defence did wrong? Put your hands up if you know.'

Karen wasn't sure, there were several

mistakes as far as she could see. She put her hand up tentatively . . .

'They were sloppy on marking!' called out Kev.

'No way! They were just too far up the field!' shouted Greg.

'Rubbish! That's not it. They just couldn't run fast enough!' shouted someone Karen didn't know.

'All they need to do is sack the goalie!' cried another. 'It's obvious!'

Karen put her hand down. They all seemed to be very definite about what was wrong, very confident that they were right. She wasn't quite so sure, so she decided to keep quiet.

They watched the film again, and again Brian stopped it and asked them to comment. The same thing happened, everyone shouted out at once and Karen didn't even bother to put her hand up. It wasn't until near the end that she decided she might as well shout out too, but she was still hesitant, her voice was quite soft and she was drowned out by the others.

'You were quiet!' Andy said as they walked out.

'Everybody else seemed to know

everything!' said Karen. 'I was only guessing.'

'So were they!' said Andy. 'At least, I was.'

'But they were so sure! They didn't say it was a guess,' said Karen. 'They made out they knew everything, and that anyone who didn't agree with them must be an idiot.'

'They didn't really know,' laughed Andy. 'It's just that no-one likes to look stupid.'

'Oh,' said Karen. 'Are you really that good on your skateboard?' she asked him.

'Yes.'

She gave him a look. 'Really?'

'Well . . . no,' he said. 'But don't tell anyone else.'

Karen stared at him. 'Is it worth lying about?' she asked.

'Well, they were all on about how brilliant they were! I didn't want to look a right wimp, did I? Do you want to play with my Game Boy? It's dual control.'

'No. I've got to go and ring my mum.'

'You haven't!' he said. 'My mum insisted that I rang as soon as I got here to let her know I hadn't been kidnapped by foreign spies, but that was it. I told her she was positively not to ring me here!'

'Well, my mum's on her own, she worries,' said Karen. 'Besides, she's dying to hear all about the course.'

'Your mum's never interested in football?'

'Of course!' said Karen. 'She goes to all my matches.'

'Unreal!' said Andy. 'See you later.'

Karen's mum was full of questions. 'Are you eating properly? Is everyone else having to share rooms? They aren't picking on you because you're a girl, are they? Are you homesick?'

Karen reassured her and then went back up to her room, only to discover that Andy was in the middle of a fight with Leroy. They looked as though they were trying to kill each other!

'Stop it!' she cried, trying to come between them, but they rolled about on the the floor, ignoring her. Finally, Leroy was on top of Andy, pinning him to the floor.

'Take it back!' he demanded.

'No!' muttered Andy.

Leroy bent Andy's arm back. 'Take it back!!' he repeated.

'OK!' panted Andy, his eyes closed. 'I didn't mean it.'

Leroy laughed and let go of his arm. Andy rubbed it ruefully, and then got up.

'What was all that about?' asked Karen.

'Leroy reckoned that I was a racist, just because I said he was the token Black on the course.'

'What's a "token Black"?' asked Karen.

'Someone who's only put on the course to show that the Football Magic people aren't discriminating against black boys,' said Andy. 'It was only a joke, to stop him going on about how brilliant he was.'

'Do you have to sort it out by fighting?' demanded Karen.

Andy and Leroy stared at her. 'What other way is there?' they asked.

'Discussion,' said Karen. 'Fighting just means that whoever is the strongest wins, it doesn't mean that they're right.'

'Get him!' said Leroy. 'Might is right, didn't you know that, Dave? Besides, fighting is fun!'

'Anyway, the Football Magic people

wouldn't have known if you were black, or not.'

'Oh, yes? With a name like Leroy?' asked Andy.

'Well, they didn't know that you or I were white,' said Karen. 'They don't care who they have on the course as long as they're good at football and they're not a girl.'

'Well, I should think so!' said Andy.

'Why shouldn't girls be on the course?' asked Karen.

'Because this is serious stuff! Girls would only giggle and mess around, and be bothered about getting their hair dirty!'

'Of course they wouldn't!' said Karen.

'Girls spoil everything,' said Leroy. 'Surely your twin's the same?'

'My what?' asked Karen.

'Your twin sister!' Andy said. 'Have you forgotten her already? She can't be that much of a pain, then.'

'No, no, she isn't,' said Karen, quickly, trying to cover her mistake. She'd completely forgotten she was supposed to have a twin. 'She's nice . . .' and then she stopped as Paul poked his head around the door and looked at her.

'Ivan Legbroke on the phone for you,' he said.

'Who?' asked Karen.

'Ivan Legbroke. He's ringing from a pay phone, so I should get a move on!'

'Oh, him!' said Karen, rushing to her feet. It was Dave. Ivan Legbroke! She laughed. Trust Dave to call himself that! So he'd rung. She was so pleased, she had so much to tell him.

CHAPTER 10

'Dave, Dave! Pay attention! Are you listening to me?'

Karen smiled to herself. Brian sounded really annoyed. Someone was going to be for it!

'And you can take that silly smile off your face!'

Karen looked across, to see who was the cause of his anger, and then she realized he was staring straight at her. Of course! She was Dave.

'I'm sorry,' she said. 'I was half asleep!'

'Half asleep!' cried Brian. 'You were totally brain-dead! This isn't a rest cure, you know. If you don't want to use your place on this course, there are plenty of other people who'd jump at the chance!'

'I'm sorry,' said Karen, going red. 'I . . . I didn't sleep very well last night.'

It was true. She, Andy, Leroy and Paul had lain awake for ages, chatting to each other. And then she'd got up really early to make sure she was dressed before the others.

'I don't want any excuses!' said Brian. 'I just want action. Now, dribble the ball down to me and then cross to Paul. Now! Not a week on Sunday!'

'Do you think he's called Brian after Brian Clough?' she asked Andy, at lunch-time. 'He's a tyrant! I don't think I've seen him smile once!'

'He just can't do it,' said Andy. 'His face is set in a permanent scowl. If he smiled, all his skin would crack and fall off.'

'Apparently, it's rumoured he was seen smiling in 1984,' said Leroy. 'When someone knocked themselves out on a goal-post. But it might have only been a grimace, perhaps he was worried that the goal-post was damaged?'

'Have you seen the photos they have up in the hall?' asked Kev. 'You know, the ones of every course. He isn't smiling on one of those.'

Karen stared at him. 'They don't take photos of every course, do they? All the people who are on it?'

'Sure thing!' smiled Kev. 'It's so that when you're famous, they can produce it and say that it's all because of what you learned here.'

'Even if you're famous because you're an axe-murderer!' laughed Andy.

'*Especially* if you're an axe-murderer!' said Greg. 'Cloughy could teach you a thing or two about that!'

Everyone laughed. Everyone except Karen. She just frowned. She didn't want to have her photo taken; she didn't want there to be any permanent record taken of her. What if Dave was famous one day, and they produced her photo? It didn't bear thinking about!

'They're doing the photo this afternoon,' said Paul, leaning across. 'They used to do it at the end of the course, but apparently one year someone broke their leg and couldn't be on it, so they take it near the start now before we can all kill ourselves.'

'Or be killed by Brian,' said Andy.

Karen tried to keep calm. She would get round it. She was so much smaller than the rest, she'd stand on the back row, behind Leroy, and no-one would know that she was there.

The photographer had other ideas.

'You! Come to the front!' he called to Karen.

She went to the second row. She could always duck down a bit at the last minute . . . The photographer was too busy writing on a board to notice where she'd gone. And then he looked again for Karen.

'You!' he said. 'Sit at the front and hold this!'

He gave the board to her. It read 'Football Magic 1997'.

'Right at the front!' he said, 'So we can see you clearly! Hold the board in front of your chest!'

Karen reluctantly did as she was told, but just as he was about to take the photo, she moved the board up so that it covered half her chin. Well, she thought, it was better than covering up nothing. The only shame was that Karen's chin was about the only part of her face that looked anything like Dave's!

That afternoon, Karen changed groups, so she was no longer with Andy. Unfortunately, Brian changed groups too, to the same group. She was determined to show him that she'd improved, but still he yelled at her. Fortunately, he yelled at everyone else, too, but not quite as much. She wondered if she was just being over-sensitive, but Kev noticed it, too.

'That Brian's really got it in for you, hasn't he?' he said.

'I can't seem to do anything right,' muttered Karen.

'Maybe it's because he senses that you're different?' he suggested.

Karen froze. 'How do you mean, different?' she asked quietly.

'Well, everyone else is big and tough and strong, and you're, well . . .'

Just a girl, Karen almost added for him.

'. . . small and wiry,' said Kev.

Karen sighed with relief, but only a half-sigh. Just because Kev hadn't guessed her secret, it didn't mean that Brian hadn't. He was definitely treating her differently to the rest, he was always watching her like a hawk, and even when she scored a goal, he found something wrong with what she'd done.

Maybe he knew that her school had submitted a girl as first choice? All the coaches had probably had a good laugh about it! Maybe he'd guessed that she was the girl, after all, but he wasn't going to let on – yet. After all, he knew she didn't want to shower with the rest. Maybe he was just going to keep up the pressure until she cracked? Well, she'd show him, there was no way Karen Tooms cracked for anyone! She'd finish the course, if he let her, and then, whatever happened next, she'd have achieved her objective, she'd have had the last laugh.

Fired by this determination, once more she put everything into the match. When the bell finally went for the end of the game, Karen felt as though her legs were going to drop off.

'David! Come here!' called Brian, as everyone else trudged wearily off the field. Karen sighed, and ran up to him.

'Your shooting's letting you down,' he said.

Karen glowered at him and bit her lip. Hadn't he been watching the game? She'd scored two goals and there'd only been five altogether! So how could her shooting be letting her down?

'I want you to try shots from different positions,' he said. 'First of all, one from the edge of the penalty area. Take the ball, I'll be the goalkeeper!'

Twenty minutes later, Karen trudged wearily into the changing room.

'Hey, you're really good!' said Leroy. He was totally naked after his shower. Karen didn't know where to look.

'How do you get those little legs to run that fast?' he said, finally wrapping his towel round himself.

'Years of practice being late for school!' she said.

'Yeah?' said Leroy. 'In that case I should be world champion!'

'Your goal rate is terrific, too!' said Andy.

'You think so?' said Karen, wearily untying her boots. 'Tell that to Cloughy!'

'And who's Cloughy?' said Brian, leaning against the lockers.

Karen went red and turned to face him. She'd no idea he'd followed her in.

'Er . . . Brian Clough,' she said. 'My favourite manager.'

'Really?' said Brian. But as he turned to go, Karen could have sworn that she saw his lips quiver, as though he was trying desperately not to smile.

CHAPTER 11

Brian, or Cloughy as he was now called, stayed totally obnoxious throughout the rest of the course. Whenever Karen changed groups, he changed with her, so that she was never away from him. And he was always criticizing her.

And then, almost before anyone had realized it, the final day had come. To Karen it seemed incredible; the course had seemed so endless, on that first, lonely day and yet it had whizzed past.

Everyone was very excited, because there was going to be a five-a-side knockout competition for the Football Magic Trophy. Cloughy put the names of the teams up on the board, and Karen was delighted to find herself with Andy, Paul, Greg and Leroy. They worked together well as a team; Greg was brilliant in goal, Paul and Andy were hard-working defenders, and, as Leroy told her at the outset, all he had to do was stand in the box and wait for the high balls to come over, for him to head into the goal.

They should have won. They would have won. They played really well, with Leroy and Karen sharing the goals between them. They had got as far as the final, and were nil–all, with only ten minutes left to play, when Andy passed a perfect cross to Karen. She headed towards the goal, with just Kev between her and the open goal. She side-stepped him, and was going past, when, suddenly, he whipped her legs from under her.

Karen had never known such pain. She rolled around on the grass in agony, and then Cloughy was by her side, gently feeling her leg.

'Ow!' she cried, as he found a tender spot.

'Hmm!' he said. 'I'm not sure if it's broken or not.'

Through her pain, Karen recalled all that Dave went through when he broke his leg: hospital, X-rays, his mum being sent for . . .

'No!' she gasped. 'It's not broken, it doesn't hurt that much!'

'Hmm. Try standing,' said Cloughy. 'I'll help you up.' He put her arm over his shoulder and helped her up. Gently, Karen tried to put her weight on her foot.

'Ahhh!' she cried, involuntarily, blinking hard. If she started to cry, she'd never forgive herself. 'I think it's just a sprain,' she said with far more confidence than she felt.

'I'm not so sure,' said Cloughy. 'I think we ought to have it X-rayed.'

'No,' said Karen, desperately. 'I . . . I just need to rest it.'

'I don't know . . .' said Cloughy.

'I do!' said Karen. 'I'm sure I'll be all right in a minute, if you could just help me to the side.' She gazed at him, pleadingly. She knew for sure that the closer they went to hospital, the more likely they were to discover her secret. And if they were to ring her mum . . .

'Would you like a stretcher?' asked Cloughy.

'No!' said Karen. 'That's a bit melo-dramatic, isn't it?'

'All right!' said Cloughy. 'Andy, give us a hand.'

With Cloughy and Andy's help, Karen hobbled to the side of the pitch, just managing not to cry out with the pain. There was nothing she'd have liked more than to be carried on the stretcher, but Cloughy mustn't realize how bad it was. They took her to the first-aid centre, where the nurse fussed around her and put her ankle to soak in a bucket of cold water. It helped . . . just a bit.

The game went on without her. Karen listened avidly to the cheers and groans of the spectators, trying to guess what it meant. Of course, Kev had been sent off, so they were both down to four each, but without Karen, and with the others worrying about her, the game was a lot more even. In the last minutes, Greg let in a goal, and they lost.

All Karen's team came in to tell her the bad news.

'There's going to be a presentation later,' said Leroy. 'We're sorry we let you down, Dave.'

'No. I let you down,' said Karen. 'I

should never have let Kevin get that close to me, we know what he's like.'

'Certifiable!' said Greg. 'I can see him making it to the top as a professional footballer.'

'How's the leg?' asked Andy.

'Throbbing like mad!' she said, pulling a face. 'But don't tell Cloughy, he'll only fuss. Where is he, anyway? Congratulating the winners?'

'No. I think he said something about going to ring your mum,' said Paul.

Karen gasped. 'No! He can't!' she said. 'Someone . . . Andy, go and stop him!'

'Why?' asked Andy.

'Um, she's got a weak heart, she mustn't have any shocks and if someone rings her to say I've hurt my leg, her imagination will go into overdrive! Quick, Andy, please!'

'It's too late,' said Andy, going to the door. 'He's coming back down the corridor. Maybe she wasn't in?'

'I hope so!' said Karen. It was her last chance. But knowing her luck . . .

'What does he look like?' she asked, quietly.

'Rather puzzled, actually,' said Andy.

Karen groaned.

'Leg troubling you, Dave?' asked Cloughy, walking in.

'No, no, it's OK,' she said, looking down. She couldn't bear to see his face.

'I've just had the strangest phone call,' he said. 'I rang your mum.'

'Oh,' Karen whispered. So she had been in. She should have known!

'I told her that you'd injured your leg, that we feared it might be broken. And do you know what she said?'

Karen shook her head, she couldn't speak.

'She said that she knew. That you had definitely broken it.'

Karen stared at him, startled.

'Is your mum . . . is your mum psychic?' he asked. 'Has she seen into the future before?'

'N . . . no,' said Karen. 'Er, did she say anything else?'

'Just something about we ought to know that your leg was broken. But without an X-ray, no-one can be sure. At least, no-one, it seems, except your mother.'

Suddenly the wonderful truth dawned on Karen. Of course! He'd rung Dave's mum and told her Dave had broken his leg! No wonder she'd told them they ought to know, she must have thought Cloughy was batty!

Karen couldn't help laughing. Knowing Dave's mum, Karen wouldn't be at all surprised if she'd called him a few choice names!

'What's so funny?' asked Cloughy.

'Did she . . . did she say anything else?' she asked.

'No . . .' he said, going red. 'Well, nothing important. Dave, is your mum ill, or anything?'

Karen started to laugh again. With a great force of effort she managed to turn it into a cough. Andy patted her on the back.

'No, no, she's fine!' said Karen, wiping her eyes. 'I think I'm coming down with a cold, though.' And she started to cough once more.

Karen managed to persuade the nurse that her leg was just sprained. It was certainly badly swollen, and the nurse dried it and then bandaged it carefully. Finally, Karen was able to hobble outside to where the presentation was about to start.

'The Football Magic Trophy for this year goes to Simon's team!' said Cloughy, and Karen joined in with the applause of the others, as they all trooped up to shake his hand, even Kev.

'Now, then,' said Cloughy. 'I don't think any of you know, but we have a special award, the Wanderers Cup, that we give to the most promising young footballer each year. Usually, we present just the Cup, but some years we come across a footballer of such promise that we arrange for him to be offered a junior coaching contract with Bolton Wanderers Football Club. Yes, Leroy, *the* Bolton Wanderers Football Club.'

Everyone laughed, nervously. They all stood stock still, staring at Cloughy, hardly daring to breathe, wondering if it might possibly be them who would be offered the contract.

'As I said, this contract is not offered every year. It is not enough to be the best on the course, the person concerned must be exceptional. Last year, and the year before, we didn't award it, but this year, I can say without a doubt, that we do indeed have someone with exceptional promise.'

Everyone smiled. Someone was going to get it. Karen shot a glance at Leroy, standing head and shoulders above everyone else. He was built to be a footballer.

'This junior contract is a training contract. Each summer holiday, the person concerned will be allowed to go to Bolton and take part in junior training. When he is sixteen, provided he has continued to show promise and dedication, he will be employed by Bolton as an apprentice. I do not need tell any of you what an honour that is.'

Karen glanced at Andy. He was so tense, standing there with his fists clenched, she knew he was willing that he would be the one. Maybe he would be; she hoped so.

'I am delighted to announce that this year the Wanderers Cup and junior contract have been awarded to David Burrows!'

Karen started to clap, along with everyone else. And then it occurred to her just who David Burrows was! Everyone was looking at her, and as for Cloughy, he was actually smiling!

Someone pushed her, and she stepped

forward, and Cloughy shook her hand. It all seemed like a dream, even her ankle didn't hurt any more. She shook her head in disbelief.

'Well done, David,' said Cloughy. He held out a big, silver Cup that gleamed so much, Karen could almost see her own stunned face in it.

'We're counting on you to show them at Bolton,' he continued. 'Don't let us down.'

'I won't,' she whispered, and then, taking the heavy Cup, she turned and faced Paul, Leroy, Andy, Greg and all the rest, and they smiled at her and clapped and cheered. Still, she couldn't believe it. She'd won the Cup, she was the best on the course. What on earth would her mum say? It might even make her speechless!

CHAPTER 12

'So that's why Cloughy was keeping such a close eye on you!' exclaimed Leroy. 'To make sure you really were as brilliant as he thought you were.'

They were sitting in the canteen having their final meal of the course. All the sessions were over, everyone would be going home tomorrow, and now, for the first time, they could relax properly.

'He had me fooled!' said Karen. 'I was convinced he thought I was totally useless. All he ever did was criticize!'

'He was testing you out,' said Andy. 'How do you feel to be winner of the Wanderers Cup?'

Karen looked at him. 'Strange,' she said.

It wasn't a very satisfactory answer, but how could she possibly put it into words? She was proud, of course, absolutely thrilled that Cloughy thought that her football was that good. But she was also very sad, because she wouldn't be able to take up the contract with Bolton Wanderers. After all, she wouldn't be able to pretend she was Dave Burrows for the rest of her life, would she? It seemed so unfair; yet again being a girl was counting against her.

'So that's Dave's future guaranteed, a pro with one of the clubs in the Premier Division,' said Paul.

'Well, only if I'm good enough,' said Karen.

'Of course you're good enough!' said Andy. 'I only wish I'd won the contract. That might at least make my dad consider me being a pro, instead of selling teddy bears!'

Everyone laughed. 'Selling teddy bears!' exclaimed Karen. 'Is that a job?'

'It certainly is. My dad owns a toy shop, and all he ever talks about is when

I take over the business! I can't stand it!'

'I wouldn't mind spending my days in a toy shop!' said Greg. 'Especially if they've got the full range of Nintendo software.'

'Oh, well, we have, but I don't get to play with any of it,' said Andy. 'I just have to stand behind the counter, smiling politely at everyone and having to be apologetic to parents complaining about how their doll's head's just come off, when all the time their little horror's been using it as a battering ram! Oh, I can't stand it!'

'Doesn't he know how you feel about working in the shop?' asked Karen.

'Oh, yes! He knows all I want to do is play football, but he has this idea that it's a bad career. He always looks on the black side: "All you need to do is break your leg, and then where are you? Out of work. At least toys give you security, people always want teddy bears!"'

'Who wants security?' asked Karen.

Andy pretended to look shocked. 'But what about when I'm married, and I have a wife and six children to support?!' he exclaimed. 'What if I can't afford to buy my children teddies?'

'He never says that!' laughed Karen.

'You should meet him,' said Andy.

'My mum's the same,' said Leroy. 'She keeps pointing out all the lads who don't make it in football, and then can't get jobs.' He put his hands on his hips and a funny expression on his face. ' "What would happen to your mortgage, then, Leroy, my son?", "How would you feed the kids?" She forgets all about the rich guys in the sport who are driving around in Porsches.'

'Mortgages, kids, it's all so heavy!' said Karen.

'Tell my mum that,' said Paul. 'She's just the same, she wants me to go into a solid, respectable job one day. What does your mum think about your future, then, Dave?'

Karen shrugged. 'We haven't really discussed it.'

'What, haven't you told her that you want to be a professional footballer?' asked Paul.

'No,' said Karen, 'but I know that she'll support me in whatever I want to do, unless it's illegal! As long as I'm happy.'

'Happy!' said Leroy. 'Is that what you're supposed to be!'

'Of course!' giggled Karen.

'If only it was that simple! The thought that I have to hold down a job for forty years scares me!' he said.

Karen frowned. She'd never really thought about it. She'd like to have a good job, but she didn't feel pressurized. She'd also like to get married one day, have a few kids, maybe take some time off work to spend with them if she found it suited her.

'I thought I might be a nurse,' she said.

They all stared at her. 'A nurse!' laughed Paul. 'A boy, a nurse! How sissy!'

Karen went red. She'd forgotten she was supposed to be a boy. It was a good job she hadn't said that she'd also thought about being a beautician.

'Caring for other people isn't sissy,' she said. 'Especially if they're very ill.'

'So you don't want to be a footballer, then?' asked Andy.

'No, well, I don't know, I hadn't really thought it was the career for me,' said Karen.

'And you've won that place at a top football team!' gasped Leroy. 'What a waste!'

'I'm sorry,' said Karen defensively. 'I didn't ask them to give it to me.'

Leroy shook his head, and everyone else looked at her accusingly. Karen felt terrible. If only they knew the truth, that at least they had the chance to try for a football club. She'd never be offered a chance at Bolton Wanderers, or anywhere else. All she'd be able to do was watch from the sidelines.

'I think if you've got a talent, you should use it,' said Andy.

'Do you really mean you're not going to take up that place at Bolton?' asked Greg. 'You're going to throw up the chance of spending the next six summer holidays practising with the best football trainers, rubbing shoulders with top footballers? And, after that, the chance of taking up an apprenticeship when you're sixteen!'

'No, no! Of course not,' said Karen, shaking her head.

'I should think not. Cloughy would be furious!'

'I just hadn't thought about what I was going to do for a job,' said Karen. 'It's such a long way ahead, so much can happen. Honestly, I'm only nine and a half!'

'My dad's always on about it,' said Leroy. He pulled a funny face and started mimicking again. ' "Work hard at school, and you'll get a good job, Leroy, my lad. You don't want to be among the millions of unemployed, do you, Leroy, my son?" '

Andy laughed. 'You should be a comedian!'

'Don't!' said Leroy, rolling his eyes. 'That's even more unreliable than being a footballer! My mum would go crazy!'

After dinner, they went to the Games Room and played pool. Karen had hardly played it before, and it showed.

'Dave wants to get on the table and start kicking the ball around!' said Paul.

'Ah, well, you can't be brilliant at everything!' laughed Leroy, as Karen finally lost with the lowest score of anyone. Her ankle was hurting her, but she didn't like to use it as an excuse.

'Count me out of the next game,' she said, and went off to find a toilet.

As she walked in, one of the canteen staff came out of a cubicle. She took one look at Karen and screamed.

'What is it?' she cried. 'What do you want?'

Karen looked at her as though she was stupid. 'I'd have thought that was obvious,' she said. If only the woman would get out of her way, she might just be able to get to a cubicle.

'I haven't got any money on me,' the woman said.

Karen stared at her. 'I don't want your . . .' she began. And then she realized the awful truth. After a week of being careful, of popping into the boys' toilet and shutting herself into a cubicle, she'd finally gone into the Ladies'!

'Oh, look, I'm sorry!' she said, and turned and walked quickly back out. Well, as fast as her ankle would let her.

As her luck would have it, Leroy was walking past as she came out. He stopped and looked at her and then at the sign on the door.

'I know!' said Karen. And she darted into the boys' toilets.

Everyone was giggling about it as she walked back into the Games Room.

'I reckon winning that Cup has affected Dave's brain!' grinned Andy.

'Yeah, he thinks he's a girl!' said Paul. They all laughed.

What's so funny about that? thought Karen, going red. She opened her mouth to tell them all the truth, but then her courage failed her. They wouldn't believe her, not at first, and then, when they did, they'd probably hate her for managing to fool them all for so long. So, instead, she pulled a rueful face and said, 'I was just thinking of other things.'

She left them to their game and hobbled along the corridor to the hall, where all the photographs were on the wall. She wandered around, staring up at all the other hopeful young faces who'd come here over the years. Below were photos of the lucky ones who'd made it into professional football. There were an awful lot of them.

She sat down on a chair and rested her throbbing ankle. She wondered how many of her course would make it, how many of future courses. Before, she'd never even allowed herself to think of the possibility for herself, but now, more than anything, she wanted to be one of them.

Her ankle ached so much, she was so

sad that the course was over, that they'd all go away and she'd never see Paul or Leroy or Andy again. Or even Cloughy. And her dreams would come to nothing. It was all too much. She started to cry.

CHAPTER 13

Karen soon pulled herself together. She told herself she was overtired. She'd been lucky enough to come, she knew that; she should look on the positive side. Poor Dave hadn't even had that chance, there he was with his leg in plaster and still smiling. She was really looking forward to see him and her mum. It would be good, as well as sad, to go home.

'Here you are!' exclaimed Andy, putting his head round the door. 'You all right?'

'Yes!' said Karen. 'I was just resting my ankle.'

'Go on! I bet you were planning where

they'd put your photo when you're famous!'

'Maybe!' laughed Karen.

'We're all going to bed now, they're shutting the Games Room.'

'Oh, OK,' said Karen, getting up wearily. 'I'd better have my bath, then.'

'Another bath! I've never known anyone have as many baths as you!' said Andy. 'You have one every night!'

'Perhaps that's my secret for success!' smiled Karen. 'I think a good soak might do my ankle good, anyway.'

'Well, don't be too long!' said Andy. 'Leroy's got some crisps and I've got a bottle of Coke, we're going to have a pyjama party!'

'Brilliant!' said Karen. 'As long as no-one expects me to dance with this leg!'

The party went on until past midnight. Andy had a radio, Leroy entertained them all with his impressions, and Paul turned out to be a brilliant dancer.

At half-past eleven, Cloughy opened the door to find out what all the noise was about, and they invited him in. As he downed a Coke and told a few jokes of his own, it seemed as though he was

119

almost human after all. But then, at twelve-thirty, he told them they had to be quiet.

'If I send you home to your mums looking shattered, they'll sue me for not looking after you properly!' he said. 'I expect to see you for breakfast at eight o'clock sharp.'

They all climbed into their beds and Cloughy switched out the light. Karen closed her eyes, but she couldn't get to sleep. She tossed and turned.

'You still awake?' asked Andy.

'Mmm!' said Karen.

'I'm not the least bit tired,' he said.

'Nor me,' said Karen.

'Did you really never think of being a pro?' Andy asked. 'It's all I've ever dreamed of.'

Karen sighed. 'I suppose I never really thought I was good enough,' she said. 'I guess if Bolton Wanderers were to offer me an apprenticeship, there's no way I'd turn it down. But then,' she muttered, 'pigs might fly!'

'What?' asked Andy.

'Oh, nothing.'

'Will you give me your address?' asked Andy. 'You could write and let me know how you get on at Bolton Wanderers. Maybe even come and stay. We've got a spare bedroom.'

'Oh . . . I don't know . . .' said Karen. This was getting very awkward!

'Well, never mind,' said Andy. 'It was just an idea.' But he sounded hurt.

'We could write anyway,' said Karen. She looked around the room. 'You know, I can't believe we only came here a few days ago. It seems like forever. That first day, I was so nervous . . .'

'So was I!' said Andy.

Karen looked at him. 'You were?'

'Why do you think I was waiting for you to get changed and come out on the pitch with me?' asked Andy. 'There was no way I wanted to walk out there on my own.'

Karen smiled. 'But you looked so cool!'

'I wasn't. I felt so scared and alone, I wondered what I was doing here, how I'd fit in.'

'Well it didn't show,' said Karen. 'I felt just the same. When you went out to play and left me to get changed, I just sat here and wanted to die!'

'I thought you were stuck-up – you wouldn't come out onto the pitch with me and you looked so upset when I said we were sharing a room.'

'I was just nervous,' said Karen.

'We've been through a lot together, haven't we? Cloughy's training schedules, canteen meals . . .'

'Kev's tackles!' laughed Karen.

'Yeah!' said Andy. 'You know, when you finally joined me out on the pitch, I thought you were a real wimp. Everyone else was saying they were really good, and all you could say was that you ran a bit!'

'I remember!' giggled Karen. 'You said you were brilliant!'

'Well, I had to, didn't I?' said Andy.

'Did you?'

'Of course! Everyone else was bragging like mad.'

'Why, though?' asked Karen.

'Well, you have to, don't you? It's like school, everyone brags on in the playground about how magic they are!'

'Do they?' said Karen, puzzled. It wasn't like that at her school.

'Yeah. Of course they do. Everyone wants everyone else to think they're the best. If you don't talk big, then you aren't big. Actually, I get a bit fed up of it.'

'I get fed up of my friends saying nasty things about each other,' said Karen. 'They can be really vicious.'

'Oh, I know a few who like to kick and punch, too,' said Andy. 'They're real bullies, and it's not always the biggest ones.'

'Oh, they don't kick!' said Karen. 'They don't do anything physical, it's the things they say! They all decide they're going to be your friend one day, and the next day, none of them are. And they say nasty things behind your back.'

'Really?' said Andy. 'You sound as though you come from another planet! What's the matter with the boys at your school?'

'Oh.' Suddenly Karen understood. Of course! She'd been talking about girls. She didn't really talk to the boys at her school, except on the football pitch. Dave was her friend, of course, and he liked to brag on a bit and throw his weight around, but only when he was with other boys, not when it was just her and him. She hadn't realized until now that boys were that different from girls.

'I haven't really got a best friend at school,' said Andy. 'Not one I can talk to the way I feel I can talk to you. I just hang around in a group.'

'Me too,' said Karen. It wasn't true; she'd got two best friends, Dave and Suzie, but she decided she'd better start acting like a boy otherwise Andy would be suspicious. She knew the boys at her school didn't have best friends either, at least none of them except Dave, and that was her, so she guessed she didn't count.

'That's why I'd like us to stay friends,' said Andy. 'We don't live that far away from each other. I'm sure you could come over for the weekend, pass on all the tips you learn at Bolton . . .'

Karen bit her lip. 'I'd like that,' she said. 'But, well, there's something about me you don't know.'

'What?' he asked.

'I can't say,' said Karen.

'Go on!' urged Andy. 'You can't just say there's something I don't know, and then not tell me! It's not fair.'

'No,' said Karen.

'Why not?'

'You might not like it.'

'Don't be daft! It can't be that terrible!'

'Oh, it isn't,' said Karen. 'But you might think so.'

'Rubbish,' said Andy. 'You don't steal off little old ladies, do you? Or rob banks?'

'No!' laughed Karen. 'Of course not, it's nothing like that.'

Andy frowned. 'Well, then, I don't see why you can't tell me! Hey, you're not a robot, are you?! Now that would explain why you're so brilliant at football!'

'Of course not,' smiled Karen.

'Well, then!' said Andy. 'What's the big secret?'

'Whatever you find out about me, you won't mind?'

'It's not going to change you, is it?' asked Andy.

'No,' said Karen. 'I'll still be the same person.'

'Well, that's all that matters, then,' he said. 'Trust me, come on, come on!'

'No,' said Karen. 'Not now. But as long as you promise me that you won't mind, you won't make a fuss, I'll write to you. Give me your address.'

'Oh, Dave! This is all so mysterious!' said Andy. 'I can't stand it! Tell me what your secret is, now!'

Karen hesitated. Could she trust him? It would be awful to spoil everything, right at the end of the course.

'No, I'll tell you in my letter,' she said.

'But I can't wait!'

'No,' she said, firmly. 'You'll just have to learn to be patient. Boys can never wait for anything.'

'Oh, all right! But what's all this "boys" business?' asked Andy, yawning. 'You sound as though you think you're a superior being.'

Karen didn't answer. She just smiled a secret smile to herself.

CHAPTER 14

Saying goodbye was hard. It seemed as though Karen had known everyone for so long, and yet, amazingly, just a week before she hadn't even met them. Leroy and Paul promised to write, and Karen gave them Dave's address and said she'd reply if they did, but she knew they wouldn't. They'd be too busy playing football.

'Will you still talk to us when you're famous?' asked Paul.

'I will, but I don't know if you'll talk to me!' said Karen, ruefully.

'I'll look out for you in the Cup Final of 2007!' said Leroy.

'Well you may not see me!' laughed Karen.

'See you! I'll say I'll see you, it'll be my job to mark you!' said Leroy. 'Just you wait!'

'Now then, you lot! I don't want you going home and forgetting all you've learned!' said Cloughy. 'I want people to watch you in action and say, "Ah, he's been on a Football Magic course!"'

'Right!' smiled Greg.

'And Dave,' he said, 'let me know how you get on at Bolton!'

'Sure thing!' said Karen. 'Thanks for all your help. You were great.'

'Great!' said Cloughy. 'I was a tyrant, I made your life hell!'

'That too,' grinned Karen.

Karen and Andy walked down to the coach stop together. It was only when they were standing there that Karen realized that they were catching the same coach. Her stop was four before Andy's.

'So it'll be easy for you to come and stay, you just get on this coach and you'll be almost at my door!' said Andy, grinning. 'What brilliant luck!'

Karen wasn't so sure.

They were worn out from the course and their late night, and even though they had each other to talk to, both Karen and Andy fell asleep on the coach.

Karen woke up first. She looked at Andy. How would he react when he knew she was a girl? None of them on the course had had anything good to say about girls, but then, she supposed that if she was with a group of girls she wouldn't have much to say that was complimentary about boys. She might want to, but all the other girls would laugh at her. Wasn't it strange? It wasn't as though they were creatures off a different planet.

Or were they? She sat back and thought about all she'd learned on the course – not about football, but about being a boy. It *was* different to being a girl, she realized that now. Boys behaved differently: they didn't support each other the way girls did. Look how desperate Andy was to have a best friend, someone he could confide in, instead of having to boast to. She smiled. It was very useful to learn that when boys appeared to be incredibly clever, they were just bragging. She'd be able to use that in the playground in future!

She sighed. Being a boy wasn't all the fun it had appeared to be. There was this career pressure thing, she was glad she didn't have that. And she didn't like the way they settled everything by fighting. But then, she wasn't too keen on the fact that girls could be so spiteful to each other. She supposed there were good and bad parts of being boys and girls, if only they could get together, see how the other half thought, maybe they could share all the good aspects? But that was as likely as pigs flying again. Or as her being able to take up her apprenticeship at Bolton.

She sat up. She was almost home. She nudged Andy in the ribs.

'Wake up, lazy-bones,' she said. 'I'm getting off in a minute.'

Andy yawned and stretched. 'When I get home, I'm going to go to bed for a week!' he said.

'You can't!' said Karen. 'It's school on Monday!'

'Don't remind me!' he groaned.

Karen got her things off the luggage

rack. 'Well, here we are!' she said.

'You will write, won't you?' asked Andy. 'And tell me your ghastly secret?'

'Yes,' said Karen. She almost fell on top of him, as the coach stopped.

'Bye!' she said. 'And keep kicking!'

'You bet!' said Andy.

Karen could see her mum waving madly at her through the coach window. She waved back, and then hobbled out of the coach. Her mum was waiting at the door.

'Karen!' she exclaimed. 'Oh, Karen, I have missed you! How are you? What have you done to your ankle?'

Karen clambered off the coach, and her mum took her things. She turned and smiled back up at Andy. But he was staring at her, his mouth open. He looked totally gob-smacked. And then she realized. He'd heard her mum call her Karen. He knew! She shot another glance at him. He was horrified! She couldn't bear to look at him. She turned back to her mum, and hugged her.

'It's good to be home,' she said. 'How are you?'

'Never mind me! How are you? What's

that bandage doing on your ankle?'

'It's only a sprain,' said Karen. 'I'll survive. How's Dave?'

'Looking forward to seeing you. Come on, let's get you to the car!'

Karen looked back at the coach. It hadn't moved, a passenger was arguing with the driver over her ticket. Karen glanced again at Andy. He looked just the same, he didn't even smile at her. She supposed it was too much to expect that he would still like her.

She hobbled along the street. All her joy at seeing her mum had vanished. She supposed there would be no point in writing to Andy now . . .

Her mum was chatting away nineteen to the dozen about all that had happened while she was away, but Karen wasn't listening. She was so angry with Andy! What difference did it make that she was a girl? Why did he have to be so disappointed? She thought she knew him, that he was above all that. She'd like to go right up to him and thump him on the nose, just the way a boy would.

Suddenly, her mum stopped talking, and Karen looked at her.

'What on earth's the matter with that boy on the bus?' she demanded.

Karen turned back to the coach, to where Andy was banging away on the window and shouting. They couldn't hear him through the glass, but when he saw her looking at him, he pointed to her and put his thumb up and grinned. He accepted her as a girl! He still wanted to be her friend!

She grinned back at him and waved. He was still waving as the coach drew away.

'What a weird boy!' said her mum, disapprovingly.

Karen laughed. 'He's OK!' she said. 'Come on, I'm dying for some of your chocolate cake!'

'You are?' said her mum. 'What on earth did they do to you on that course?'

'They gave me a Cup,' said Karen, smiling, and looking a bit embarrassed.

'What?' Her mum almost dropped her bags. 'A Cup! What was that for?!'

'Being the best on the course,' said Karen.

'What?!' exclaimed her mum. She did drop the bags then and threw her arms around her daughter. 'Wow! Brilliant!

Fantastic! Oh, darling, I'm so proud of you!' she exclaimed, and twirled her around in the street, in front of everyone. People stopped and stared, and Karen went bright red. She knew she should have waited until she got home before she told her mum!

CHAPTER 15

As soon as she had dropped her things off at home and had something to eat, Karen went to visit Dave. He was as thrilled as her mum that she'd won the Cup.

'And no-one found you out?' he asked. 'You managed to convince them you were a boy for the whole of the week?'

'Yes,' smiled Karen. 'I made a few mistakes, but they were all so convinced that girls can't play football, that they didn't suspect a thing.'

Dave shook his head. 'Well,' he said, 'I never imagined you'd do it. I was so worried, I thought that any minute my mum was going to come striding in and demand to know what was going on. She did have a rather weird phone call from the Football Magic people, though!'

Karen laughed, and explained what had happened.

'That was close!' said Dave. 'So where's this Cup?'

Karen took it out of her bag and gave it to him.

'Wow!' he said, breathlessly. 'That's some trophy!'

'It's yours,' she said.

'What? You'll keep it for the year, won't you?'

'Oh yes!' said Karen. 'Mum's cleared a space on the mantelpiece for it already. But your name will go on it when it goes back to Manchester.'

'I suppose it will, won't it?' said Dave. 'I wish I could have gone on the course!'

'Never mind,' said Karen. 'I've got something better for you.'

'What?'

'How would you like to spend your summers training at Bolton Wanderers?'

'What?!'

She explained about the training contract. 'There's no way they'd take me,' she said. 'I can't go on pretending I'm a boy. They're expecting a Dave Burrows, so that's where you'll be going every summer from now on.'

'I can't!' said Dave.

'But you must, otherwise it'll be wasted.'

'No!' said Dave, shaking his head vehemently.

'Why not?'

'Because you won it, I didn't! I can't have your place, they'll realize I'm not that good.'

'Nonsense!' said Karen. 'You were second-best in our school trials, weren't you? It was only because you co-operated that I got to go to Football Magic, anyway. You should have gone, you would have done if you hadn't broken your leg. So this is my way of saying thank you.'

'But I *didn't* go to Football Magic, that's the point! You've learned so much in that week, I'll never catch up with you now.'

'I'll teach you!' said Karen. 'As soon as you get that leg out of plaster, we'll have training sessions.'

Dave shook his head. 'I'm not going,'

he said. 'It's great of you to offer Kaz, but I wouldn't be able to relax or enjoy it. I'd be terrified they'd find me out.'

Karen shook her head. It amazed her that a boy who had no fear of swinging upside down from a bar over two metres from the ground, was frightened of playing a little trick, especially as it meant he'd be able to train at Bolton Wanderers.

'Listen,' she said, 'if I can spend a whole week pretending to be a boy, then surely you can go to these training sessions, pretending nothing?'

'Nothing except being brilliant at football.'

'But you are!'

He shook his head.

'My place will be wasted, then,' she said. 'And the chance of an apprenticeship at sixteen. They won't give it to anyone else on the course.'

'Looks like it,' said Dave.

Karen glared at him. He could be so stubborn!

'Hello, there!'

Karen looked up. Mr Jay was standing at the bottom of Dave's bed.

'Hi!' she and Dave said together.

'New hair-do?' he said, looking at Karen. 'I hardly recognized you!'

'Oh, um, yes,' she said.

'And it looks as though we've got two invalids here! What happened to you, Karen?'

'Oh, I just hurt my leg playing football. It's only a sprain, unlike Dave.'

'So I see!' said Mr Jay, looking at Dave's plaster. 'That looks rather painful.'

'It's getting better,' he said.

'It's a miracle he didn't break his neck!' said Karen.

'That's not the only miracle around here!' said Mr Jay. 'Wait till you hear this one! I understand that you went on the Football Magic course, Dave. And not only did you play, but you won the Cup for being the best player! Ah, I see you've got it there!' Mr Jay picked up the trophy. 'And all with a broken leg! I must say, I find it totally and utterly amazing!'

Karen and Dave looked at each other guiltily.

'It was my fault,' said Karen quietly. 'I tried to contact you to find out who should go on the course in Dave's place, but you'd gone away. We may have lost the place in future years if we didn't send anyone . . .'

'So you went in his place,' said Mr Jay.

Karen nodded her head. She couldn't look at him. 'It was nothing to do with Dave,' she said. 'He didn't want me to do it, he said I'd get found out. But he couldn't really stop me, not being stuck in hospital with his leg in plaster.'

She paused, waiting for Mr Jay to lay into her, tell her how she'd ruined the reputation of the school, but he didn't say anything. Finally, she raised her eyes to his. And then she realized that he was trying not to laugh. At the sight of her face, he couldn't help himself. He burst into gales of laughter. Karen smiled uncertainly, and looked at Dave, who was smiling too.

'I think it's fantastic!' Mr Jay said, when he finally stopped.

'You do?!' gasped Karen.

'To take Dave's place, to make everyone think you were a boy! I don't know how you managed it!'

Karen laughed. 'It had its sticky moments!' she said.

'And to win the Cup as well! That was your undoing. Brian, the senior coach there, rang to tell me the good news, but when I spoke to your mum, Dave, she was mystified. She told me about your leg, and that Karen had gone on the course in your place. I must say, when I told Brian, he was speechless!'

'You told him,' whispered Karen.

'I rang him back this morning. You'd just left.'

'Oh,' said Karen. 'I bet he was mad! Oh, I can just imagine it! I feel terrible.'

'Oh, he saw the funny side in the end. He told me to tell you that he thought you'd put on a brilliant performance!'

'Really?' said Karen, smiling with relief.

'And what's more, he said that if you're an example of how well girls can play football, he's going to allow girls on his course in the future!'

'He is?' said Karen, her eyes shining. 'That's fantastic!'

'So you've really achieved something, there, haven't you?'

Karen smiled. 'I have, haven't I?'

'There's one thing I don't understand, though. How were you going to keep up the annual training sessions at Bolton? And then the apprenticeship?

You weren't going to pretend to be a boy for the rest of your life, were you?'

Karen frowned. 'No. I offered it to Dave, but he wouldn't take it.'

'I should think not. It's your place. And it seems as though Bolton are going to let you go along next summer, even though you're a girl.'

'They are?' gasped Karen. 'No kidding?!'

'No kidding,' said Mr Jay. 'Brian rang them this morning, and it seems they decided that all the publicity of taking a girl would be good for the club.'

'Brilliant!' said Karen. 'Me, train at Bolton Wanderers!'

'Magic!' said Dave.

'They might possibly let you go in future summers, too,' said Mr Jay. 'Mind you, you won't be able to take up the apprenticeship. After all, they don't allow women in the Football League, at least, not yet.'

Karen pulled a face.

'But then,' smiled Mr Jay, 'they did say that no girls were allowed into Football Magic until you came along, didn't they? And look what you did there! Who knows what other barriers the irrepressible Karen Tooms might break down?'

Karen smiled happily at him. He was right. With the right attitude, some luck and a lot of determination, she felt as though she could do anything, anyone could. So the League didn't allow women footballers, eh? Well, she'd just have to see about that!

THE END

SOCCER MAD
Rob Childs

'This is going to be the match of the century!'

Luke Crawford is crazy about football. A
walking encyclopedia of football facts and
trivia, he throws his enthusiasm into being
captain of the Swillsby Swifts, a Sunday
team made up mostly of boys like himself –
boys who love playing football but get few
chances to play in real matches.

Luke is convinced that good teamwork and
plenty of practice can turn his side into
winners on the pitch, but he faces a real
challenge when the Swifts are drawn to
play the Padley Panthers – the league
stars – in the first round of the
Sunday League Cup . . .

0 440 863449

CORGI YEARLING BOOKS